About the Author

I was born and raised in Manchester before studying for a Forensic Science degree at Staffordshire University. I eventually moved to South Wales where I met my husband and became a full time mum to my three children, Emilie, Morgan and Osian. Health Issues forced me to rethink my path in life and reawakened my long, lost passion for writing.

Millie's Adventure
Chasing Rainbows

Laura Thomas

Millie's Adventure
Chasing Rainbows

Olympia Publishers
London

www.olympiapublishers.com
OLYMPIA PAPERBACK EDITION

A CIP catalogue record for this title is
available from the British Library.

ISBN: 978-1-78830-648-5

This is a work of fiction.
Names, characters, places and incidents originate from the writer's
imagination. Any resemblance to actual persons, living or dead, is
purely coincidental.

First Published in 2020

Olympia Publishers
Tallis House
2 Tallis Street
London
EC4Y 0AB

Printed in Great Britain

Dedication

To my beautiful daughter, Emilie, for being my inspiration, for always being humble and teaching me how to always be strong.

Emilie
Instagram: @emilie_violet_allen

Chapter One

The Competition

Millie had been doing gymnastics for almost five years and this was the first year that she would be competing at national Compulsory Level. She had just competed at her pre-national's friendly competition but it had all gone horribly wrong!

The week of the competition, Millie's ankle had been hurting in training. Not hurting so bad that she couldn't walk on it, but a strange kind of hurting that she couldn't explain. Because this was Millie's first competition outside of Wales, Millie's mum and dad had booked a hotel for the night as a treat, and so that Millie could get a good night's rest before her competition. The day of the competition, Millie's ankle was still hurting as she got ready to head to the gym. She had done a few of her basic stretches at the hotel but couldn't stop the aching. As soon as the car pulled up outside of the gym, the nerves kicked in and Millie began to cry. Before she left the car, Millie's mum had to remove her earrings. The emotions were all too much for Millie and she cried uncontrollably whilst her mum tried her best to calm her down, whilst trying to remove the earrings. Finally, the earrings were out, and they could get out of the car!

As she stepped onto the floor for warm up with her team mate and coach, Millie looked uncomfortable. Her usual bouncy spark just wasn't there. Her parents could see it, her coach could see it, but most importantly the judges would also see it. First up was beam. Shoulders slumped and head down, it started well as Millie got up on to the beam and began her routine. She walked stiffly across the beam with a forced smile on her face and took a deep breath as she prepared for her first big skill… the dreaded backwards walkover. She had been having so many problems in training as Millie had developed a mental block and a huge fear of going backwards on the beam. In training she had just started to overcome this fear, and although she was just starting to put her skills back onto the floor beam, the thought of doing them up on the high beam filled her with dread. Each one she did in warm up she fell, and Millie was nervous, no not nervous, she was scared of doing it… here goes… nailed it! Millie couldn't believe she had stuck it. The look on her coach's face was one of surprise and happiness. Next up was her full spin… and she fell. She had done this move a thousand times in training and could stick it with her eyes closed. Pain shot through her ankle as she got back up on the beam, tears flooding her eyes, but she carried on. The last thirty seconds flew by as Millie walked and shimmied her way across the beam ready for her big dismount cartwheel tuck back off the beam. As she fought back the tears, Millie had never felt such relief to have that over with. Millie's coach put her arms around Millie and at once she felt safe, but she couldn't relax for too long as next up was floor.

The other girls were taller than Millie and were so graceful as they moved across the floor, performing each move effortlessly. Everyone always said that Millie was like a little doll, she was short and had a tiny frame, nothing like the tall, long limbed girls that surrounded her. Millie sat watching from the edge of the floor with butterflies going crazy in her tummy. Finally, it was Millie's turn, but she looked pained as she took to the floor with a limp in her step. Again, the nerves were obvious to everybody watching but as her music started, Millie started to relax into her routine. As she bounced across the floor, she stuck all her tumbles. Her spins were far from graceful, especially as it was her lead ankle that was hurting, but she got around and got the marks. At best, the whole routine was scruffy. There were no big mistakes, but she didn't feel happy, if anything she felt disappointed with herself.

Range and conditioning was up next. This had always been Millie's weakest piece. Although she appeared to be flexible to the untrained eye, her flexibility wasn't as good as she wanted it to be, as good as it needed to be, despite hours and hours of stretching in the gym and even being stretched by her coaches. As she took to the floor once again, Millie took a deep breath as she went into handstand. Her mum couldn't watch as she rushed through the routine. Just as she had done on floor, no mistakes but rushed and still not happy. Vault came and went with very little drama and last up was bars, which was Millie's favourite piece, and at least she wouldn't have to use her ankle, except for the landing. As hoped, the routine went well without any mistakes and Millie was happy with her bars performance, but overall, she still felt disappointed.

The medals ceremony was predictably miserable for Millie as she already knew she hadn't performed her best, and her face showed exactly how sad she felt inside. After the medals had been handed out, the gymnasts were given a copy of the overall scores and rankings. No surprise to Millie, her name was down there at the bottom… she was last overall. Millie's little brother, James, was the first to throw his arms around Millie when he saw her, and her mum and dad both told her that they were proud of her. As Millie and her mum looked over the scores on the long journey back home to Wales, her mum began to giggle. Millie looked confused for a moment, and then she saw it too. She might have come last overall, but she hadn't come last in the dreaded range and conditioning. OK so she was second to last… but that wasn't last! It had always been a joke in Millie's family that the biggest achievement in any competition was not where she came overall, but that she didn't finish last on range. As she thought about her competition, she felt at ease knowing that her parents didn't care how she had performed, they were just happy knowing that she had tried. Millie couldn't help but smile and giggle to herself every time that she thought about her range score. It was such a silly thing but to her, she had found the positive in what had been a very negative competition. Liz, Millie's coach, was OK about her routines, and how she performed, but they both knew that there was lots of work to do before nationals.

Chapter Two

The Ankle

Back in the gym on Monday, Millie felt down. Everything was going wrong. Her ankle was still hurting, and her head was not in the right place. Millie had been to see the doctor that morning about her ankle, who examined it but just said to take it easy. Not something you tell a gymnast who is determined to be in the gym, but the doctor felt that as there didn't seem to be any damage to her ankle, light training wouldn't make it any worse. After an hour and a half, Liz decided to give Millie the rest of the night off, and as Tuesday was her rest day anyway, it would hopefully give her ankle time to settle down.

Wednesday came and Millie's ankle was hurting badly. Half way through training, Millie's coach called her mum in to the office and Millie's heart sank. It was never anything but bad news when parents were called into the office, especially when it was half way through a training session! Liz explained to Millie's mum that it was not unusual for gymnasts to start to get aches and pains in their ankles as the new moves that Millie was learning meant using different muscles to what are usually used. Liz didn't think it was anything too sinister, but because of where Millie was complaining of it hurting, something just didn't seem right. They decided that the best thing to do would be for Millie to get checked out by the hospital, just to be sure.

At the hospital, Millie and her mum waited in the waiting room for what seemed like hours. Finally, it was Millie's turn to see the triage nurse and tell the whole story. Millie told the nurse how she had first noticed it aching but not hurting when she was in gym. She told about the new skills that she was learning in gym, and then, reluctantly, Millie told the nurse about the incident in the park. She had been messing around with her dad and her brother, James, who was nearly two years younger and was playing on the roundabout. Whilst she was spinning around, Millie stuck her leg out and "CRACK" she hit the side of her ankle against her dad's leg. This was the first time Millie had told anyone about this incident as she didn't want to get her dad in to trouble, but this was the first time that the pain had started to get bad. Millie only saw her dad every two weeks, that's if her dad was around to see her and her brother, so she didn't want her mum to be cross that they had been messing about, even though deep down she knew her mum would just be pleased that she was spending time with him. Accidents happen after all!

The nurse reassured Millie that everything was probably fine, just a sprain, but that they would do an X-ray just in case. Millie went in to the room with the radiographer who took the X-rays whilst her mum waited outside. She was a nice lady. She talked with Millie and told her that she had been a gymnast when she was younger, and then had become a cheerleader.

After another long wait, Millie was finally called in to see the nurse again, who had a picture of her ankle on her computer screen. The nurse didn't look quite as happy as she had before.

"I'm really sorry but it's bad news, you have broken your ankle."

There was silence in the room, nobody could believe that

1. the ankle was broken,

2. Millie had not only been training with a broken ankle for over a week, she had competed at her last competition with her ankle broken.

"We need to put the leg in plaster and then get you seen by the doctors in fracture clinic in a few days when they will put a new cast on. You MUST NOT put any weight on your ankle for the next few days until you see the doctors."

"You are very brave, Millie," the nurse continued, "In fact, you are the only person that has walked into the emergency room all day without hopping, and is leaving with a plaster cast and crutches!"

Millie didn't really know how she felt, there was a mixture of emotions bubbling up inside. One thing was for sure, she would not be competing at nationals in a few weeks' time, but she didn't know if she felt happy with relief that the pressure had been taken away, or sad that she would not get the chance to compete at the level that she had worked so hard for over the last few years.

The next day, Millie's mum took her in to gym on her crutches to see her gym friends, and whilst she enjoyed the attention that they showed her, she couldn't help but feel sad.

Liz said that once Millie had seen the doctors and had her new cast put on, she could come in to gym and work on her strength and conditioning, and of course her beloved bars. For the next four weeks, Millie continued to go into gym and worked hard on her strength and conditioning skills.

The time finally came for Millie's cast to be removed and Millie could not wait to get back in to the gym properly and start regaining all her skills. The first few sessions went really well, then out of nowhere, the decision was made that Millie could not go back into the gym without a letter from a doctor or physio. Millie was so upset but her mum told her not to worry, that she would do her best to sort it. Unfortunately, it wasn't quite so easy. The doctor at the hospital had told Millie that she should completely rest her ankle for the next three months to make sure it was completely healed.

The next thing her mum tried was their own doctor, who had previously told them that there was nothing wrong. No luck. They wouldn't do anything because she had been seen by the hospital. Millie's old coach worked at the local university and was herself a physiotherapist. She recommended a good physio for Millie to see. The physio was a kind lady, not very old, with a nice smile. She had worked with lots of gymnasts before, including some of the Olympic gymnasts, who Millie looked up to and wanted to be like. The physio showed Millie's step dad how to tape up her ankle and said after a week, that Millie could return to training. However, gym was not happy with Millie having her ankle taped, and said she could not return until she could train without it being taped.

Millie was feeling so sad that she felt that she no longer wanted to go back to gym. It was time to quit. But what next? The thought of quitting was bad enough but not doing anything at all filled Millie with so much dread that she didn't know what to do. Millie loved gym more than anything in the world, but she had also enjoyed spending time at home with her family, something that she didn't get to do very often. Millie was a young carer for her mum who was disabled, she had an illness which Millie couldn't pronounce, and nobody had ever heard of anyway. On the bad days, Millie helped around the house or helped with her youngest brother, Sean, who was only a baby. Millie didn't mind at all, in fact she enjoyed having her family so close around her when she was at home. So many of her friends had parents who worked and spent very little time with them that Millie was grateful to have her mum and step dad at home with her and her brothers. And what about Portugal? Millie had been lucky enough to have been chosen to attend a training camp in Portugal with six of her team mates. Her mum had spent so much time helping to fundraise for the trip that Millie felt like she was letting her down. But even more than that, Millie really wanted to go to Portugal!

Over the next week, Millie thought about the radiographer whom she had seen at her hospital, the one who had also been a gymnast… and then a cheerleader. As Millie thought about this, she remembered that two of her friends in her class at school had recently started cheerleading. Maybe, just maybe, there was something that Millie could do after all.

After thinking some more, Millie decided to speak to her mum and step dad about the idea. As they all sat in the kitchen for a rare family meal together, Millie decided it was now or never.

"Mum… Dad… I've been thinking. Instead of going back to gym I would really like to try cheerleading."

As if they had read her mind, Millie's mum said, "That's funny, because that's something that we wanted to talk to you about!"

It turned out that Millie's mum and dad (who was really her step-dad, but she always called him Dad) were so desperate for her not to give up on her talents that they had also been looking for other sports for her to do, and had also come up with cheerleading. After much discussion Millie and her parents agreed that she would go back to gym for six weeks to make sure that quitting was the right thing for her to do, and at the end of that six weeks, the local cheer team, Allstars, would be holding their annual open training taster sessions ready for the next cheer season. Whilst Millie had been off gym, her mum had been working hard, desperately trying to get physios and doctors to give her the all clear to go back training… and now the time had come to go back!

At her first training session back, Millie felt nervous and scared and didn't want to go in, but with the help of Liz and all the girls, those nerves soon melted away. She was back where she belonged, at the place she loved, with her friends, working hard on her strength and conditioning, and soon had many of her skills back, maybe not exactly as good as before, but they were there. Before she knew it, six weeks had passed, and it was time for Millie to decide. Now that it came to it, she didn't want to quit, but she still wanted to explore cheerleading. Surely it wouldn't hurt just to give it a try. Millie went to the first open taster session, and just as she thought, she loved it! The cheer coaches were all very impressed with her flexibility... in gymnastics this had never been her strong point but the fact that she could easily do over splits was a very big bonus. She even got a mention on the club Instagram and Twitter! This was the confidence boost that Millie needed!

Just to make sure, for the next three weeks, Millie continued to train at gym to get back up to full strength and attended the weekly cheer taster training sessions every Sunday. Every week she would be with a different stunt group and every week she would learn new stunting skills, but those four weeks went by too quickly and it was now time to decide. But what should that decision be? Millie so desperately wanted to start cheer training, but she was also really starting to enjoy gym again too, she had her passion back for the sport that she had loved for most of her life, how could she just walk away from it without it leaving a huge hole in her heart?

Chapter 3

The Trial

Millie didn't know it, but her mum had secretly been speaking to the cheer coaches to try and find a solution that would keep everyone happy, especially Millie. The next Tuesday Millie's mum took her down to the cheer studio for an individual assessment trial to see what skills she had, and which team she could join if she chose to start cheer.

Millie was so nervous. As she walked into the gym Atomic were training. This was the team that everybody wanted to be in. They were overall Grand Champions at all the major events and were also going to be performing at The World Championships in Florida next year. Millie clung hard to her mum as she watched them flicking and twisting all over the floor! Millie knew instantly that is where she wanted to be. Not only did she want to be a part of Allstars cheer, she wanted to be Allstars Atomic. She wanted to be performing all these amazing moves, she wanted to perform on the world stage!

Millie's mum bent down and whispered, "You can do this, I believe in you. Show them what you can do."

Head coach, Natalie, took Millie over to warm up at the side of the floor. She nervously looked back at her mum, who smiled and gave her a nod... she could do this! Once she had warmed up Natalie introduced Millie to Allstars tumble coach John who had been a part of Atomic for several years. He was also a part of Team Wales and had represented club and country at the European and World Championships. John was only young, and he put Millie at ease straight away. To start, John took Millie through some of the basics. Handstand forward roll, cartwheel and round off. Easy, thought Millie. Next, John asked Millie to do a Y-stand. Millie had never heard of this before, it wasn't a gymnastics term that she was familiar with. She didn't want to tell John that she didn't know what this was, instead Millie froze. Natalie sensed that Millie didn't understand what this move was and stepped in. She explained to Millie what it was and asked John to demonstrate, almost immediately, Millie once again relaxed. Of course she could do a Y-Stand!

Next, John explained that he wanted to assess some of the more difficult moves, and not to worry if she couldn't do a move or if she needed support. Millie took a deep breath. Focus. First up was round off flick series. As Millie took to the floor she smiled to herself, she could do this.

Another deep breath, and she ran into a round off and performed a beautiful flick. Natalie and John looked at each other and smiled approvingly. Next up was round off tuck back which again Millie performed beautifully, but the trial wasn't over. With every move, Millie was feeling more and more confident in herself, and next up was the final part of her trial... standing skills. Millie wasn't quite sure what this meant but was buzzing with excitement. John asked Millie if she could do an aerial. Millie smiled to herself, she was just putting her aerial back on to beam, of course she could do it on floor. Here goes, she thought... and she landed it perfectly. Next, John asked if Millie could do a standing tuck back. Millie froze. Before breaking her ankle, Millie had been learning standing tuck backs in gym as a bit of fun at the end of training, to break up practising the same boring competition routines for hours at a time. But she hadn't done one since she had been back at gym. John must have sensed her unease as he asked Millie,

"Do you want me to support you?"

"Yes please," smiled Millie, suddenly feeling confident again. Confident and determined.

To begin with, John allowed Millie to have a few practice goes jumping from a block like she was used to doing in gym. After the first two, Millie was feeling more and more confident and was happy to move to the floor. John supported her as she jumped backwards. Perfect. John asked Millie if she wanted to have a go on her own. She nodded. She was unsure if she would manage it, but she felt confident and knew that John was there to help if she needed it. Millie took a deep breath, counted to three... counted to three again and jumped. She jumped as high as she possibly could before bringing her legs up above her head. Before she had even landed, she knew she had done it. As her feet hit the floor, Millie had the biggest smile on her face as John gave her a high five. And just like that, her trial was over.

Natalie came over to speak with John and her mum whilst Millie sat and watched Atomic. They were doing the most amazing stunts. Some looked quite scary and very dangerous, but Millie knew that this is where she wanted to be. She wanted to fly just like these girls!

In the car on the short ride home, Millie's mum explained that both Natalie and John had been very impressed with her skills and would be happy to have her join Allstars, and better still, Millie could pick which team! They had taken away with them a copy of the team training packs which explained a bit about each team, which skills were needed and, most importantly, training times.

As she read through the pack, Millie was on a high… this is definitely where she wanted to be, but what about gymnastics? The more Millie thought about it, the more she realised that she wouldn't even have been given this opportunity if it wasn't for her years of gymnastics training. And with her sights set firmly on the future, Millie knew that she still needed to learn more tumble skills to progress to Atomic as soon as she was old enough. And what about her friends? She knew that she would make new friends in any cheer team, but she wasn't ready to leave her gym friends behind. The more she thought about it, the more she realised that she needed gymnastics in her life. But then something hit her like a bolt of lightning out of nowhere… cheer had given her the confidence to face her fears and put gymnastics skills onto the floor that she hadn't done in months.

The following day at gymnastics, Millie couldn't shake off the feelings of happiness from the night before, feelings that she hadn't felt in the gym for a long time. Even Liz had noticed how happy she was, bouncing about like her old self. And her confidence was back. She wasn't afraid to try new skills any more. Millie was so happy coming out of gym, but also full of nerves as she knew what she had to do.

"Mum… I've been thinking, I was wondering if there is any possible chance that I could do gymnastics AND cheer?"

"I thought you might ask that!"

Millie's mum had seen the bounce back in her step and had watched her smile grow with every training session. She had spoken to Liz about how gym had been going and, just as she had expected, Liz confirmed that Millie was back to her old self and, if not, even better than she had been before. She was focused, she was determined, and most important of all she was happy. The decision had already been made for Millie to drop down from Elite Grade to National Grade as she had missed so much time off from training which seemed to also take away a lot of the pressure, adding to her happiness in the gym. Mum had spoken to Liz about Millie wanting to start cheer, thinking that she would be happy and supportive, but Liz was not overly happy at all. She had seen it before, gymnasts had started cheer in the past and had become sloppy, developing bad habits as cheer and gymnastic tumbling are slightly different. But it was this new found love of cheer which had got Millie back in the gym to begin with.

The next thing to do was look at the cheer teams. Whilst Millie was still doing gym, that would have to come first, so they had to look at when the cheer teams trained. Millie's only days off were Tuesday and Sunday, although she did finish gym at five thirty on a Thursday. When Millie joined her new gym club on a Thursday, she started missing half a day of school so she could attend gym at one thirty. This was all dependent on her keeping good grades in school, but strangely, Millie's grades improved! So, Thursday evening was also a possibility for cheer training too.

Natalie had emailed Millie's mum with a list of the cheer teams that Millie could join based on her age, and had said that they would really like her to join Angels, which was Junior Level 3. This was amazing news, but there was a problem. They trained on a Wednesday evening when Millie was in gym. Liz had already expressed her unhappiness about Millie joining cheer, but if it meant that cheer would keep Millie in gym then her mum didn't care, she just wanted Millie to be happy. So, the only option that was left that wasn't a basic skill level was Junior Level 2 Comets.

Millie's mum emailed Natalie to explain that the only option really was for Millie to join Comets, and Natalie was more than happy to have her. The next email read: *Congratulations, Millie, and welcome to Allstars Comets. We will be looking forward to you starting training with your new cheer team after the summer break.*

Good Luck!

Chapter 4

Portugal

Summer break at cheer also meant that it was time for Millie's training camp in Portugal. It was Friday night in gym and they had one more training session to go before the girls left for their big adventure. Liz had let the girls have an unusually long break when suddenly, they heard a strange noise coming from outside the changing room door. In came Liz, followed by all the girls' mums carrying great big sports bags. Liz explained that local businesses had very kindly donated kit for the girls to take out to Portugal with them, and because they had done so well with their fundraising, there had been enough money left over to buy them all matching clothes for travelling and training in. The girls were screaming with excitement, they all felt like superstars!

Sunday finally arrived, and as Millie pulled up to gym with her family, she saw the bus and the other girls waiting for her. Suddenly, the excitement was hit with a sense of sadness. She was really going to miss her family, she had never been this far from home without them before. Millie hugged her brothers and squeezed her mum and dad tightly before joining the other girls on the bus. They were all giddy with excitement in their brand-new matching outfits. The girls waved goodbye to their parents as the bus pulled out of the car park, and Millie settled into her seat. After everything that she had been through already this year, breaking her ankle, the ups and downs and the wanting to quit gym, the fear of leaving this amazing group of girls for the unknown of a new cheer team. The new adventures that cheer would open to her. Right now, in this moment, Millie was happy, she was content with how things were working out for her.

The journey to Portugal seemed to take forever. The drive to the airport was quite long and the girls spent most of the time singing away at the top of their voices to each new song that came on the radio. Liz and two other coaches, Danielle and Mike, were travelling to Portugal with them, and once they had checked in at the airport, they headed straight for the fast food counter! The girls didn't have to wait long until their flight was called, and they headed to the plane.

Millie was so excited, she loved flying, but her friend Tia had never flown before. Tia was scared. Millie held Tia's hand as the plane took off and before long, they both settled into their seats. It was only a two-hour flight, so it wasn't too long before the plane touched down in Portugal. The excitement was more than the girls could contain!

The training camp was a short bus ride away and the girls were all starting to feel very tired. Back home it was ten p.m. so the coaches let them have a quick supper from the canteen and showed the girls to their rooms. Being the youngest, Millie and Tia were sharing a room with Danielle. At least they would both feel safe at night having an adult in their room, whilst the slightly older girls shared a triple and double room. They were happy to have a bit of freedom away from any coaches. For the next week, Millie and her team mates worked hard inside the gym, but they also played hard too! Every day started with an early breakfast around seven a.m. before hitting the gym for the first of their two daily training sessions. Training was hard. The girls were taught new skills as well as working hard on the basics. After lunch the girls were allowed free time… this meant hitting the pool. Millie knew she couldn't swim very well. She had lessons when he was younger, which she had really enjoyed, but her parents could no longer afford to pay for the lessons, so she had had to stop. Now she was beginning to feel nervous. She closed her eyes, held her nose and went for it… SPLASH! Millie felt the cool icy water cover her body, she had done it, she was in! Millie had always loved being in the water, and now she seemed to have found a new confidence pushing her to swim more and more. Every day, the girls were allowed free time to use the pool and, by Wednesday, it was hard to keep Millie out of the water, which was a good job as Thursday was nearly here. As a special treat, Thursday was beach day! After breakfast, the girls boarded the bus which took them on a small tour of the city. The driver didn't speak very good English and the girls were all far too excited to get to the beach to listen to what he was saying. As they left the bus at the beach, the coaches took the girls over to pick up their wetsuits. The girls were confused. It was boiling hot outside why would they need wetsuits? Mike told them in a fit of excitement, that they were off to surfing school! A pang of dread and fear hit Millie. Over the past few days her confidence had really grown in the water, in fact she was always first in the pool and last out, but this was different. This was the open sea!

As the lesson started, Millie relaxed and started to enjoy herself. She wondered if she looked as silly as everyone else jumping about on their boards on the sand, but she didn't care, Millie was having too much fun. It didn't seem to be too long before the instructors told the girls to head for the water, and as the cold salty water gushed over her feet, Millie was no longer afraid of the water, she was happy to be learning new skills with her friends. Just as Millie had suspected, she wasn't very good at surfing! No matter how many times she tried, she just could not stand up on her board whilst catching the waves. Although she had enjoyed the lesson, Millie was glad when it had finished so that they could have some free time and fun at the beach. The girls had all been given a small amount of spending money which was left over from their fundraising. Once they had finished at the beach and before they headed back to the bus, Liz and Danielle took the girls to have a look around the shops. There were lots of little stalls all along the edge of the beach, the type of stalls that you only ever see on holiday, all selling lots of different, weird and wonderful things. There were dolls wearing strange fancy dresses, and the same dresses were available to buy in children's size. There was a stall selling grains of rice with your name on it, encased in glass and hanging on a necklace. There were all sorts of bracelets and ladies doing hair braiding. And then they spotted it. Claire's was stood on the corner just calling to them to go inside. As they passed through the doors from the blistering heat into the cool air-conditioned store, they were in girly heaven. Surrounded by hair bows and bracelets and every kind of accessory imaginable. They had flown all the way to Portugal to spend all their money in a shop that they could have visited in Cardiff! It didn't matter. Millie and her friends only had two more days left before they flew back home, and they would be taken up with training.

On the last full day in Portugal, the camp had arranged for a big farewell disco for all the girls who had attended from around the world. This was the day that they were all looking forward to most, and it was also the day that Millie had packed most of her clothes for. Wearing leotards all the time, Millie just didn't feel right in anything that wasn't leggings. And she didn't get too many chances to go places to get dressed up. Millie was nervous as she didn't want to dress over the top, but she did still want to make an effort. She tried all her different outfits on, and paraded up and down the corridors between all the older girls' rooms in the search for fashion advice. In the end, Millie discarded all the brand-new clothes that her parents had bought her especially for the trip, and went with her favourite orange dress. Mille had first got this dress last year as a treat for doing well in a gymnastics competition. She wasn't so sure about it to begin with, but over time it had grown on her, so much so that it was her favourite go to dress for any occasion... weddings, christenings, parties, or just a Sunday stroll in the park. The disco was, at best, OK, and the girls soon decided to head down to the pool area where they could still hear the music but could also play at the pool table. Nobody really knew how it happened but suddenly there was a great big SPLASH! Out of nowhere, Millie had jumped in to the pool fully dressed. Everyone turned around to see Millie in the middle of the pool in fits of laughter, and before she knew what was happening, the other girls had followed suit and were also jumping in the pool after her! It was certainly turning into a leaving party that none of them would forget!

The following day was half a day by the pool before they made their way home. Millie had enjoyed her time away with her friends, she had enjoyed meeting new people and learning new skills, but she was looking forward to seeing her family. She hadn't spoken to her parents the whole time that she was away, and to be honest, she couldn't say that she had missed them. But now that it was time to go home, knowing that in a matter of hours she would be reunited with her family, her heart ached for them. Millie so desperately wished that she had a time machine that she could just fast forward and be back in her own home, with the people that mattered most to her. Instead, she would have to endure two bus journeys and an airplane ride home first.

Chapter 5

New Beginnings

Now that Portugal was over, it felt to Millie like a whole new start… A new beginning. In gymnastics, Millie knew that there would be change. She knew that she would have to step up her training as she would be competing at National Grades in the following spring, and although it was slightly easier than National Compulsory Levels, she still had to be able to do the skills, and she had always liked to make sure she had a few bonus moves thrown in too! The first training session back, Millie was focused and ready to get to work, but someone was missing, her partner in crime, whom she had bonded so well with in Portugal, Tia, wasn't at training. Millie thought maybe she was just having an extra day off as they had only been back from Portugal less than forty-eight hours. After a week of full on intensive training in Portugal, the first session back was an easy, fun filled, session to settle them all back in to routine. It was a beautiful, hot, sunny day, just like they had in Portugal, so Liz even allowed the girls to have their breaktime snack outside. It had only been a day, but Millie missed the girls when they weren't around and was so glad to be back training. They shared their stories of Portugal with the younger gymnasts, who had been too young to go. Since moving to her club just over a year ago, Millie had been lucky enough to attend several training camps in the UK, and each time she had always been the youngest. She looked up to the older girls so much, and in turn she knew that she also had a responsibility to set a good example to the younger gymnasts. The girls sat and told stories of the last night disco, and training and learning to surf at the beach, but Tia's absence was noticeable, especially to Millie. After training, Millie's mum and dad were in the car to pick her up. Usually it was just her dad, but Millie didn't question it, she was happy to see her mum.

"How was training?" her parents asked at the same time!

"Fine," replied Millie, "But Tia wasn't in tonight"

"Ah, I know," replied mum, "Tia isn't coming back to gym any more, she has decided to try a different type of gymnastics at a different club."

Millie's emotions were running high. She had just had an amazing week away, she had just had a fantastic training session, and now she was being told that she wouldn't be seeing someone who had been like a sister to her for a long time. Millie lived a long way away from gym and even further away from where the other girls, especially Tia, lived. It wasn't like she could just see her whenever she fancied. Millie couldn't contain herself as the tears began to roll down her cheeks and she began to sob uncontrollably.

"Hey, don't cry," Millie's dad tried to lighten the mood. "Just think, you will be meeting your new team mates for the first time tomorrow in cheer."

This made Millie cry even harder. She had missed the very first training session as it was the day that she was travelling home from Portugal. She kept thinking "what if they have made friends already" or "what if they don't like me". And to make matters worse, the day after, was also the first week back at school.

Millie didn't mind school, in fact she quite enjoyed it. She was popular with almost everybody, but there wasn't really anybody that she could say was her close friend. When she first started in nursery, there had been a few of the girls who had become close and had spent quite a bit of time together. Unfortunately, there were several factors that pulled them apart, firstly that her mum couldn't attend the social events that many of the mums held regularly, and that pushed Millie out of favour. Secondly, Millie didn't live near any of the other girls and with her gym commitments, she couldn't just hang out whenever she felt like it. Nevertheless, Millie was in no way unpopular, she was the sort of girl who was everybody's friend. This year, Millie had a new teacher to the school, Mr McElroy, whom she had briefly met last term. The head teacher had introduced Millie personally as Mr McElroy was big into sport, so who better than Millie to show him the ropes. Millie bonded straight away with Mr McElroy, but the first day back in school was Thursday, her half day of school in favour of gym training, so Mr McElroy would have to manage by himself. Millie was happy coming out of school having seen her school friends, who retold all their stories of foreign holidays and fun family days out. She was happy to be going training with her besties, even though seven was now down to six.

Training was very quiet for a Thursday as there were only five of them in. Millie thought that maybe Hanna wasn't in training because she couldn't get out of school, especially with it being the first week back. Four hours seemed to fly by, maybe because they were having too much fun, or maybe because Millie couldn't stop thinking about the upcoming cheer practice... she was counting down the hours, and then the minutes. Before she knew it, it was the end of the session and Liz called everybody to line up, just like she did at the end of every session. She didn't know why, but Millie felt that something was different.

"Good training session, girls... Good work girls, blah, blah, blah."

And then it hit them. Millie watched the words flow from Liz's mouth without really taking them in.

"I'm really sorry, girls, but Hanna won't be coming back to train with us any more, she will be moving to Dragons Gymnastics."

The tears stung as they rolled down her face and as she looked around, she wasn't the only one with puffy red eyes and tear stains on her cheeks. Millie felt that this was yet another blow to her, a very big stab in the heart. Hanna had been like a big sister to them all, why didn't she tell them she was going? First Tia, now Hanna, how many more of her gym family would be leaving her? On her way to cheer, Millie didn't really know how she felt. She was sad at the news of the girls leaving, she was filled with nerves at the thought of walking into cheer on her own and not knowing a single person. She felt sick. Very, very sick. And to make it all just that little bit worse, she already knew that she would be late!

Natalie already knew that Millie would be late for training on Thursdays as she finished gym training at five thirty and started cheer at six. In theory there would be no problem, except that it was a forty-minute drive from gym to cheer on a good run, but Millie would already be warmed up and ready to go when she got there so Natalie said it was fine. Besides, Natalie really wanted Millie on the team so was happy to make a compromise. As Millie walked through the doors at Allstars cheer, she clung to her mum, there were people everywhere. There were people coming and going from the previous classes, there were people at one end of the floor doing tumble and others in the middle of the floor doing separate warm up. As they made their way to the changing rooms, Millie asked her mum how she knew where to go, they had never been in here before. Millie's mum smiled, "This is where it all began."

Millie looked at her confused, "What do you mean?"

"This is where your gymnastics all began, this was your first club."

"No, it wasn't, Fusion was my first club" Millie replied, still looking very confused.

Millie had been to a few clubs over the years. She had left her old club, City Gymnastics, a year and a half ago when she moved to Vale Gymnastics. She had been happy at City and she adored her coach, Amy, who was an amazing coach and such a nice person. She always made training sessions fun for them, letting them try new things. Millie was the youngest of all the girls, which is the way she liked it. They would do circuits and weightlifting and CrossFit, which Amy loved to do and so did the girls. Slowly, one by one, the older girls in her squad left to join the national training squad, which frustrated Amy who spent years nurturing each girl, coaching them to be champions, to then have them taken away from her. Amy eventually made the decision, when there were only a few girls left, that she had lost her passion for the sport. She decided it was time to leave to follow her own fitness goals and make a career in CrossFit. Amy and Millie left simultaneously, but Millie settled in straight away with Team Vale and knew that was where she belonged. Prior to Millie joining City Gymnastics, age four and a half, Millie had been at Fusion. This was her first real taste of squad gymnastics. She had moved to recreational gymnastics when she was three and a half and as soon as she had turned four, she was taken into a squad. Millie was the youngest by two years, so the girls that she was training were more advanced both in gymnastics and in years. Millie found it difficult and felt very alone to the point where she just did not want to be in the gym at times. It was at this time that Millie moved from Fusion to City Gymnastics. And that was as far back as Millie could remember. Her gymnastics journey had in fact started at Allstars at the age of three. At that time, Allstars were just starting out in a new purpose-built gym, and although it was all very new, so were the groups and the coaches. Millie showed potential even at such an early age, but as time went on and the groups became bigger and bigger, Millie had less and less time doing gymnastics and more time waiting around. In any case, they didn't have the level of coaches that were required to take Millie further in her gymnastics, so she moved to Fusion.

After a very brief explanation, Millie's mum said, "So you see, you are back where it all started, it's fate, it's meant to be!"

Millie left her drink and clothes in the changing rooms and held her mum's hand tightly as they walked back to the floor. Natalie was busy taking warm up and as soon as she saw Millie, she rushed over smiling.

"Welcome, Millie, come and meet your new team."

Millie hadn't noticed the group of girls stretching playfully in the far corner of the floor.

"Girls, this is Millie and she is your new flyer, she has never done cheer before so please look after her!"

The girls introduced themselves in turn: Lucy was the oldest and team captain, followed by Jodie, Alys, Kaydee and Belle. Story of her life, Millie was once again the youngest. The girls were all super nice and made Millie feel welcome. She only had an hour left of training so coaches, Gina and Sarah, went through some basic tumbling. By the end of the session, Millie felt at home. She was not just happy, but glad to be there, thankful to be able to call herself a member of Allstars Comets. Millie walked out of the gym, got in to the car and threw her arms around her mum.

"Thank you," she said.

Millie's mum didn't need to ask how it had been, she could tell by the smile that was on Millie's face the whole way home!

Chapter 6

The Training

Millie couldn't wait to go into gym the following day and tell them all about her first session at cheer. She wasn't sure if her friends were particularly interested, but she just couldn't help it, she talked and talked and talked! She had already spent all day talking cheer with Emma and Naomi in her class at school, who had also just found out what team they would be in.

"Millie, stop talking and get on with your work," Liz interrupted. Oops!

It felt strange to Millie not having Tia and Hanna in gym, and even though she was sad, a part of her certainly felt sad, a bigger part of her couldn't help but be filled with happiness... she was bouncing! On break, Liz came over to sit with the girls.

"So, how was cheer last night, Millie?"

"Oh, no, please don't ask her that, she hasn't stopped talking about it since she got here," Menna replied.

Millie blushed, her face felt like it was on fire, and all she could manage was a simple, "Good!" She felt embarrassed talking to Liz about her new found love of cheer. She felt like a traitor, like she was letting Liz down or betraying her somehow. She tried not to let it bother her and before Millie knew it, it was Sunday again. It was a week since she had left Portugal, the last time she had seen Tia, and today was her first full on training session as a member of Allstars Comets.

If she was being honest, Millie had already forgotten the names of the girls in the group, but when she walked in to training and sat down with the girls, something seemed unfamiliar. She looked around, counted the number of girls that were there, one, two, three, four, five, six, seven, eight. There were two more girls than there were on Thursday, but she wasn't completely sure which two were the new faces.

"For those of you who don't know, this is Danusia and Coco."

To compete, Comets needed eight people minimum to form two stunt teams. Danusia and Coco, the most beautiful sisters ever, were experienced flyers, Coco with Ivy and Danusia was about to start her first year with Atomic, but they had agreed to join Comets as bases, 1. for the experience, and 2. most importantly, for the team to be able to compete. Introductions over, Gina gave the girls their positions, Millie was to be a flyer. When thinking about cheer, it had never occurred to Millie to be anything but a flyer, not because she thought she suited the role, but because it seemed the more attractive. Millie hated being the focus of attention, so it sounded ridiculous for Millie to be the one everyone focused on, but to Millie, it was the most glamorous. Besides, Millie was shaped to be a flyer. She was small, no, she was tiny. Although she had just turned nine she still wore age four–five clothes, but she had the shoulders of a ten-year-old thanks to gymnastics building muscles upon muscles! She was so small and light she was easy for anybody to throw around! Having never done a team sport, it was at that moment that it hit Millie just how important every member of the team was, because without her bases supporting her, there would be no flyer!

During her trial sessions, Millie had learnt some of the basic stunts, but this was a whole new ball game. In two months' time, Comets would be taking to the stage for the first time as a team for the big showcase performance. That meant not only did they only have two months to get to know and trust each other, but to learn all the stunts which Millie had no idea about: tumbles, which luckily Millie could do as close to perfect as needed, and then put them all together as a routine to music. Millie suddenly felt out of her depth, especially as dance had never been her strong point! The first thing that needed to happen was obvious... Team Bonding Session!

Chapter 7

Team Bonding

If you thought that it would be easy enough to get eight girls together from the same cheer team for a team bonding session… you would be very wrong! Because of training on a Sunday afternoon, they had the option of a Sunday morning or a Saturday. Danusia and Coco trained with their other teams on a Sunday morning, so that was a Sunday out. Saturday it was, but that wasn't easy either! Danusia and Coco had been selected to represent Wales at the World Cheer Championships in the USA, where they would take on the best in the world. Although the teams only trained once a month, they were on different teams, which meant two different Saturdays were out. The next available Saturday Millie was competing at a friendly competition, her first competition since breaking her ankle, so that was out. The following Saturday, there was a two-hour window between Millie finishing gymnastics training and Danusia and Coco's Worlds training, so it was decided that it had to be then or not at all!

Because they were so limited on time the parents decided bowling would be the best thing for them to do, which was perfectly fine with all the girls. Millie's mum asked Liz if it would be OK for her to finish training an hour early to allow her time to get home and change before heading out to bowling. Liz was happy, she had always been happy for the girls to take time out for themselves when needed. Millie was so excited as she picked out her favourite pair of leggings which she always wore. Mum had straightened her long hair the night before as a special treat. Millie's golden-brown hair was down to her bum, and it was naturally curly which very quickly turned to either very knotty curls, or lots of frizz. Because her hair was so long, she always had it tied back out of the way for school, gym and cheer training. For gym competitions, her hair was always up in a bun and for cheer, it was a high ponytail with curls. But Millie's preferred hairstyle for everyday was two French plaits. In gym, she still had to tie them together on bars as her plaits were still too long and would get caught on the bars as she was going around. So, today for training, with her hair newly straightened, Millie wore her hair in a bun that could be easily taken out when she got to bowling.

After gym, Millie protested as Mum wanted to go home first for Millie to get changed. She was already wearing her favourite top and leggings and she wanted to go straight there. Millie's mum went straight up to Millie's room, followed by a very sulky Millie, to have a look through the wardrobe to pick out something to wear. The first thing Millie reached for was the safety of her orange dress.

"No way are you wearing that. It's not appropriate and you ALWAYS wear that! You have so many nice clothes that you have never worn, let's choose something new."

"Fine," replied Millie in her finest, sulky, strop voice.

Mum just ignored her and carried on going through the wardrobe. Fifteen minutes later and ten outfit changes, Millie's mum gave in and Millie went for, not the orange dress that had been banned, but her second go to outfit — an all in one suit and a little denim jacket which she had never seen before and wasn't quite sure where it had come from. A quick brush through her surprisingly still straight hair and she was ready to go, wearing her purple high-heeled ankle boots which her dad hated with a passion.

Thanks to the little fashion crisis which had just occurred Millie was the last one to arrive, not late, but perfectly on time. Millie was never early to anything! Because there were eight of them, they had to split into two teams. They decided to split into their stunt teams: Jodie, Danusia, Coco and Belle on one team, the other team was Lucy, Kaydee, Alys and Millie. Millie wasn't very good at bowling, but she didn't care, neither were the others! They had the bumpers to make it easier for them, but still they weren't very good. For the whole of the game the girls did not stop laughing, and Millie really started to feel like she was a part of a cheer family. After the bowling had finished, the girls spent a little time playing in the arcades on the games. The DJ had started to play some loud music and in several of the more popular songs, the girls would spontaneously start dancing! The DJ noticed the girls and asked what song he should play next. Naturally, there was only one song to play... their cheer song! As soon as it came on, the girls burst into their cheer routine, singing at the top of their voices. Before they knew it, people had gathered round to watch them, some were even recording it on their phones… they couldn't stop now! They improvised slightly on the tumble sections of the routine, replacing the full-on round off flick series for a simple aerial as the space they were in was so small. Next part of the routine was stunting.

"Can you do this?" Lucy whispered to Millie.

She shook her head, lifted her leg, and she was up in the air! They did a few simple stunts and then her and Belle formed their pyramid and posed for pictures for the crowd and their parents. As the song finished, the crowd clapped and cheered and all the girls could do was giggle with excitement. Who would have thought it, their first public performance in the middle of the bowling arcade! But they didn't care, they had enjoyed themselves and they had enjoyed the attention. For the whole car journey home, which Mum was thankful was only a short ride, Millie did not stop talking. She recalled the whole event repeatedly, and even though Mum had been there and watched the whole thing, she just listened, smiling to herself at how happy Millie was.

Chapter 8

Gymnastics

For the next few weeks, cheer training was going nicely, the team coming together and learning their new routines. Gym, however, was busy with competitions. Because Millie had missed National Levels due to her broken ankle, she could enter the Voluntary Regional Grades. Although this was a lower grade than what she had been training for, it would still be difficult as the judges would be looking more at the attention to detail, every unpointed toe and bent knee would mean marks off!

The first of Millie's competitions was a friendly competition designed to be a warm up competition ready for Regionals the following week. There were girls there from all over Wales, and some of the girls were from her old club. Millie was so happy to see her old friends and, even better, she was in the same round as them so would get to go around the competition with them. Millie's old head coach was less than friendly, no doubt still upset about Millie's departure from the club, or maybe it was she never actually smiled anyway. Either way, Millie didn't care. Millie's first piece was beam. She stepped up, presented to the judge, and as she went to get on to the beam she fell! As she placed her hands on the beam and jumped, she misplaced her footing and somehow ended up still holding onto the beam, hanging upside down! Thank goodness it was only a friendly competition. The rest of the routine went really well and she was happy. Millie's other pieces: floor, vault and bars all went as well as she could have hoped for and going in to the medal ceremony, Millie felt pleased with herself. And the best part of the overall competition for Millie... Liz carrying Millie's bag around for her!

First to be announced was vault.

"In fourth position from Vale Gymnastics is Millie."

That was fine, Millie was happy with that. Her coach had played it safe with an easy vault so as not to cause damage to her ankle.

Beam next, Millie already knew that she didn't stand a chance thanks to her fall. Millie was too busy talking to the girl next to her, whose name she didn't know but she had seen at other competitions. She could see Liz waving at her, doing a strange pointing dance...

"Millie," the announcer was calling as she looked up.

"In third place, is Millie from Vale."

Seriously, third place, Millie couldn't believe it. A very happy although slightly embarrassed Millie, bounced over to the podium to collect her medal. It just went to show that a mistake, however big, isn't the end of everything! She couldn't believe that even with a fall she had come third. As she sat back down, Millie made sure to pay attention this time to the announcer. As she announced the floor results Millie listened closely.

"Sixth place… fifth place… fourth place."

Millie felt a little deflated. She didn't expect to do well on floor as it wasn't one of her strongest pieces.

"And your floor champion, is Millie from Vale."

The announcer made eye contact as she said it as if to say, "Are you listening this time?" and Millie jumped from the floor onto the podium. She couldn't believe it, first on floor! She looked at Liz, who's smile confirmed that she wasn't dreaming. Bars were next, and although she wasn't the sort of person to show off, in herself she knew that bars were her strongest piece. In fact, she was the only person who had managed to make it up into handstand without any problem, which she knew would give her bonus marks.

"Your bars champion, is Millie from Vale."

Again, Millie jumped up and smiled. This medal didn't feel quite as good as the last one as she half expected to make top three in bars, in fact Millie had never come anything but first, or at worst, joint first on bars in any competition since she had started competing three years previously. After posing for photos the girls turned to step down. Millie could feel the excitement building inside her. She knew she would be in the medals for overall, she hoped it would be gold, it should be gold…

"And your overall champion from the Vale is Millie."

Millie smiled so hard that her face hurt. She stood on the podium whilst everybody clapped, people taking pictures on phones and cameras. She went to step down as Liz shouted, "Stop!" Liz was Millie's very own paparazzi! She was always taking photos of the girls in training, so why would this be any different. After photos on the podium, there were photos of Millie sitting on the beam, team photos and any other photos Liz could think to take! Finally, Millie was able to grab her things and head over to her parents. Her brother, James, was first to greet her with his usual hugs, and as she reached her parents, (mum, step-dad and real dad), she heard all three of their phone's ping in unison. It was Liz, quick off the mark as always, and had already put Millie all over the club's social media pages! She felt like a little superstar! Unfortunately for Millie, there was no superstar celebration as she still had an hour's drive home and homework to do! Her mum promised that they would go out for a nice family meal the following weekend after her next competition.

That next week in gym Millie was bored. She was happiest when she was learning new skills or working to perfect something, but all she did was practice, practice, practice all her routines that she had competed the previous weekend, ready for the next competition. She also knew that all the other girls would also be working hard to perfect their routines ready for Regionals, so although Millie was quietly confident, she couldn't afford to let her guard down! She still had to put the work in.

The day of Regionals arrived, and Millie felt unusually calm. Normally, she would feel a mixture of excitement and nerves, but all she felt was calm. The competition was in the same place as the previous week's competition, so Millie knew that all she had to do was go in and do last weekend all over again. And that is exactly what she did! Strangely, Millie was on the same rotation as last week, which she was starting to prefer. After all the previous issues that she had on beam, she always felt happier to get it over and done with. As she stepped up to the beam she smiled, she was not going to make the same mistake again. And she didn't. In fact, she performed her routine as near to perfect as was possible. Vault, floor and bars all went well, and Millie knew inside that she would be off to Finals the following week, even before the medals were announced.

And she was right. Fourth again on vault, but this time she was champion on bars, floor and beam, and All-Around champion. To make the competition even more special, her team took the gold medal. After such a difficult year so far, Millie was starting to feel hopeful, but more than that she was thankful. She was thankful to all the people who had believed in her and pushed for her to continue in the sport that she loved. Thankful for being allowed to explore other opportunities whilst still doing gymnastics. She was thankful for the friendship that had got her here, and she was thankful for cheer! She had grown in confidence so much since starting cheer when it came to putting her tumbles to floor. Often in cheer, she was expected to tumble in trainers on a hard floor instead of bouncy like her gym floor. This had meant making slight adjustments, but they had really helped her floor routines, and her recent success proved it. The following week was just a repeat of the last, although Millie knew that she would have to really put the hard work in this week as the competition on Saturday was Regional Finals. it was the best girls in the whole of Wales getting together to battle it out. And it wasn't in any old gym, it was to be held in the National Sports Institute Arena. It sounded scarier than it was, and Millie had competed there before so already knew what to expect. Millie didn't know the other three girls in her team, but she was so used to competing on her own, that she wasn't going to let that phase her. Besides, Millie knew that the only person that she really had to beat was herself. She was focused.

Millie recognised a few of the other girls from other teams, some of them had been at her first competition two weeks ago, but the other girls she didn't recognise. There was one girl however, representing another area, who she was all too familiar with, Sophie. Millie didn't really know what to make of Sophie, she was a good gymnast and seemed like a nice enough person, but there was just something about her. She was a very beautiful girl. She had the whitest of blonde hair and such a pretty kind face, but something wasn't right, Millie couldn't put her finger on it. She seemed the kind of girl who wanted to be your friend to put you down to others. But Millie knew all too well to just play along, be nice, and concentrate on her own performance. And that was exactly what she did. Although she was feeling tired from doing three competitions in three weeks, all the hard work and training leading up to each competition and the extra training sessions that she had taken on with cheer, Millie knew that this was what it was all for. This moment right here. On each piece of apparatus, Millie performed her little heart out, she knew that every pointed toe and straight knees would be all that separated the top gymnasts. She only had one shot. She also knew that the outcome of this competition would decide whether Liz would allow her to step up to National Grades next year.

Millie performed well and went clean on every apparatus and as all the girls lined up for the medal ceremony, her heart pounded so hard and fast against her rib cage. Millie had no idea how she had done compared to all the other girls, but she did know that she had done her best. As they announced the vault medals, Millie's name wasn't called out. She began to feel sick. The floor results were called out and as they called fourth, she started to feel dizzy, had it all gone horribly wrong, but then she was heard her name called out in third place. Not a bad start, she thought to herself, knowing that beam wasn't a particularly strong piece but her trusted bars was also still to come.

"Beam... sixth... fifth... fourth... third." Millie's heart was in her ears

"Second place, Millie from Vale." She couldn't believe it! She kept her fingers crossed for bars, but she needn't have bothered

"Bars Champion, is Millie."

That was one gold, one silver and one bronze. Millie reckoned it was between her and Sophie to become All Around Champion. By now, Millie's knees were starting to wobble, she preferred when she had known she had performed rubbish, the waiting and expectation were painful!

"Second place, Millie from Vale, and in first place and your overall champion, Sophie."

As Millie stood there, she felt a mix of emotions. Obviously, she was happy to be second in Wales at her grade, it was a huge achievement, but she couldn't help feeling something that she wasn't used to feeling, she felt jealous. Of all the people to beat her, it had to be Sophie. But she smiled for all the photos that the official photographer wanted and did the usual good will hugs with Sophie and the other girls. Heading towards her parents was the same routine as always. James there first with a great big hug, photos with her brothers, and then the best bit... ice cream. As promised, they all went out for a celebratory meal. Millie's godmother had brought her daughter, Evie, to watch so Millie and Evie spent the whole time chatting. They didn't get to see each other very often as they lived in different villages and went to different schools so when they got together, they would spend the whole time giggling. Millie was six weeks older than Evie and they had known each other most of their lives. They weren't quite one year old when their parents met very randomly at the local doctors' surgery one January morning. They had got chatting and Evie's mum, Cherry, added Millie's mum on Facebook, and they had been friends ever since! They were the sort of friends that didn't see each other very often and they never spoke on the phone ever, but they communicated through Messenger every few days and were always the first to be there for each other in a crisis! Evie had a little brother, Oscar, who was three and so cute. Millie loved them all so much and loved the time she spent with them, but she always felt that it was never enough... she always wanted more time!

Chapter 9

Showcase

With all her gymnastics competitions over and done with for the season, Millie could relax a little and concentrate on her cheer routine ready for Showcase, which was rapidly approaching. She was really enjoying her cheer training and had settled in well with the other girls. The hardest part for Millie was Thursdays, going straight from four hours of gymnastics training and trying to get to cheer practice not too late! Overall, training was going well, but there were just a few minor issues with a couple of the stunts that they hadn't been hitting consistently. Showcase was here so they would just have to go out there and do their best. For a few days before the competition, Millie and her mum had been doing hair and makeup trials. They both couldn't believe how much preparation was involved in just getting ready for a cheer competition. With gym, it was just leotard, check, hair in a bun, check, handguard bag, check. Job done.

Cheer was a whole other ball game! First thing on the list was fake tan. Millie's mum had persuaded her not to bother with fake tan as it was only Showcase, and Millie was happy to oblige as she had never had it before, and with her sensitive skin and eczema, she didn't really fancy being covered head to foot in brown gunk. Second thing on the list was hair. This was a super high ponytail with as much extra height as possible, with loose curls on the bottom and a very big white sparkly bow on top like a present! Third on the check list was makeup. Lots and lots of makeup. The brief was silver sparkly eyes with black on the outside, light rosy cheeks and dark pink lips. Considering Millie's mum hadn't had an occasion to wear makeup for years, not only did she not have the experience to apply makeup, she didn't own any! All the makeup she did have got ruined when Millie decided to do her brother James' makeup some years back, and there was no point in replacing it.

So, Millie may have become a cheerleader, but her mum now had to become a hair stylist and makeup artist overnight. Because Millie's mum was having a bad flare up, she couldn't go out to the shops to buy new makeup, so off went Millie's dad, armed with his list of essential makeup items to see what he could pick up in town. Millie was so grateful to her dad (step dad) as he did so much for her and her brothers.

Millie's real dad had left when Millie was nearly five and her brother James was almost three. Millie's mum was quite poorly at the time and it was rough for all of them. Millie's mum met her new husband, Millie's step dad, a year later, and he filled a very big hole in her life. In fact, she couldn't remember a time when he wasn't in her life, and although she still saw her real dad, it was a different type of bond. Millie loved both of her dads dearly, but with her step dad she always felt more comfortable. She saw her biological dad only every other weekend and even on those weekends, it was her step dad, whom she now called her dad, who would pick her up from her dad's flat, drive her to gym, wait four hours and then drop her back to her dad's again, unless he was at rugby then she would have to wait at home until he was finished. With her step dad, she always felt she could talk to him about anything. She talked to him about boyfriends, even though she didn't have one now, and things that were worrying her in gym or at school. So, adding personal shopper onto the list of taxi driver, chef and cleaner, wasn't such a big deal.

After receiving the haul of makeup from her dad, Millie and her mum decided that Thursday night would be their first makeup trial run. Dad wasn't quite sure which shade of foundation to go for, so took a guess and then bought two anyway just to be on the safe side. The first one was so pale that it made Millie look ill, whilst the second made her look orange! With a bit of trial and error, Millie's mum mixed the two together to try and come up with something more appropriate. So that was the foundation sorted, next thing to tackle was the eyes. Again, to play it safe, Millie's dad had come up with two options. The first option looked very promising, it was a silver glitter eyeliner type gel, but as soon as Mum applied it to Millie's eyelids, they stung really bad. The second option was loose white/silver powder which looked so pretty in its little tub. This was going to be the better of the two options, but how were they supposed to get it to stick to her eyelids? In the end, they decided to use a mixture of the two, a light coating of the glitter gel and then stick the eyeshadow on top. Sorted!

Saturday arrived, and Millie was feeling excited but sick with nerves. She was so scared about performing on such a big floor in front of so many people, with all eyes on her! Millie had to be at the stadium for four p.m. and so would have to leave at three p.m. to make sure that they got there on time. It was a good job Millie was awake early because at eleven a.m. Mum shouted Millie to start getting ready! The first thing that they would have to do was Millie's hair. Mum had bought her a curling wand, which she didn't really know how to use but was going to give it a go. Millie and her mum had watched a few videos on YouTube on how to do the perfect cheer hair, so Mum was feeling quietly optimistic. Millie tried not to shout out in pain as her mum brushed and yanked her hair into a high ponytail. After three failed attempts, Millie's hair was somewhere close to where it needed to be. Now she understood why she was getting ready so early.

The next thing to do was curl the mass of frizz that was tumbling down Millie's back. It took a few attempts for Mum to figure out how to use the curling wand in Millie's hair, but eventually she got the hang of it. Forty minutes later, Mum finally finished the last curl. As Millie looked at herself in the mirror, she hardly recognised the person staring back. She looked so different and she hadn't even put her make up on yet. She swished her head back and forth, watching the curls bounce. Her hair looked so short... and so tidy! Suddenly, Mum realised, how was she going to get the bow in without spoiling the curls? Rubbish, lesson for next time, put the hair bow in before curling hair! Mum battled with the mass of curls and finally managed to get the bow in place, slightly wonky, but it was secured on top of her head where it needed to be! By now it was twelve thirty, Millie couldn't believe how long it had taken just to do her hair! Next up was makeup.

Millie hoped that the makeup side of things wouldn't take too long, but she was wrong. By the time Mum finally managed to find a shade of foundation that resembled a soft glow rather than bright orange, Millie's face was plastered with foundation. She hated how it felt on her skin. "I'm never going to wear makeup when I'm older," she thought to herself. They still weren't one hundred percent sure how they were going to tackle the eyeshadow issue. Millie typed in 'cheer makeup' into YouTube on her mum's phone and found a video which promised a step by step guide for what they needed. Mum followed each step exactly as directed. First, she applied the black to the corners of the eye, and then the glitter gel and powder. A bit more blending and they were somewhere near how they should look! The lipstick was again a mixture of pencil, lip stain and a different colour gloss to make it not quite so bright. This time, when Millie looked at herself in the mirror, she didn't quite know what to make of herself. She didn't really like it, not like she thought she would, she looked so different. Mum sensed that something wasn't quite right and said she would feel better once she had her cheer outfit on and the whole look was complete.

Aw rubbish, how were they supposed to get the teeny-weeny uniform on without destroying the hair and makeup that had just taken so long to do? Mum thought to herself that they really should have thought about it a bit better. After lots of tugging and pulling and shouting, they finally managed to get the leotard part on over Millie's head without too much damage to the hair and makeup, but Millie was on her own for the next bit…poppers.

Millie was so used to wearing an all-in-one leotard that she stepped into and pulled upwards. This was a pull over your head and fasten underneath with poppers… which also meant wearing pants, something that she never usually wore with her gym leotards. It seemed like an age of fiddling about before Millie finally managed to get the poppers to stay closed. It felt so uncomfortable, especially with her skort on over the top. This time, when Millie looked at herself in the mirror, she felt something that she hadn't felt before, she felt proud. She was proud to be part of a team, to wear a uniform and to perform with her friends, knowing that it was a team effort, everybody relying on everybody else.

Luckily for Millie and her mum, whilst they had spent the last few hours getting her ready for her first ever cheer performance, Dad had taken control of the house. He had fed the boys, changed the baby, made snacks for the car and done the dishes! They were ready to go! The car journey seemed to take forever, although it was only an hour. Millie was quiet the whole way. The nerves were starting to kick in as she was going over her routine in her head. James tried to speak to Millie, but she didn't want to talk. He turned around in a huff whilst she continued to stare out of the window at nothing. At the stadium they had to park in the multistorey car park. That was fine as everyone else was, but suddenly Millie began to feel self-conscious. There were people all around her in cheer uniforms heading to and from the stadium, but Millie felt embarrassed. She looked so different to her usual self that she didn't want to be seen out in public in her uniform.

"Stop being so silly," Mum said, getting annoyed. "How do you expect to get up and perform in front of everybody if you won't get out of the car!?"

Mum was right, this was silly. The last few weekends she had got up in front of lots of people and jumped and flipped across a tiny beam, of course she could do this. Millie pulled herself together and got out of the car.

"Hold your head up high, shoulders back and smile... and most of all enjoy it!"

And that's exactly what she did!

As soon as they entered the stadium, Millie saw her team mates and ran over to them. She looked so tiny stood next to the older girls. Millie's mum looked around the stadium, and when she looked back to where the girls had been standing she saw them all running off into the distance together. The next time that she saw Millie was as her and her seven team mates ran on to the centre stage. They were all holding hands with big smiles and even bigger bows! As the music began to play, the crowd started to roar with excitement. Millie's mum and dad watched as the girls bounced and flicked around the stage, and then came the stunts. Millie's mum struggled to watch as Millie was lifted into the air by her bases, and as they threw her up and caught her in basket. She thought watching gymnastics competitions was hard, but this was unbearable! Her heart was pounding against her ribcage and she felt sick to the bottom of her stomach. The only way Millie's mum could bring herself to watch was through the corner of her eye through her phone as she filmed it, with the intention of watching it back once it was all over. As the performance ended, the audience went wild. This was a team who last season had come bottom of every competition, and who very nearly didn't even get to perform due to lack of numbers, up on stage smashing their routine. At that moment, every parent and coach began to feel very excited and hopeful for the future of the team!

As soon as the girls jumped off the stage, Millie ran over to her parents and threw her arms around her mum so tightly that both of their eyes began to well up with tears. Millie was so happy and enjoyed every second of her performance, whilst Millie's mum felt so proud of just how far Millie had come.

Chapter 10

Christmas Break

Christmas break, for the last few years, had meant four full days off from gym if she was lucky. This year, Liz had decided to give the girls a full week off, and with two weeks off from cheer, Millie's family decided to make the most of the time and have some quality time together. As a surprise, and as part of the children's Christmas presents, their parents had arranged a family trip to London. Millie and her brothers had only been to London once and that was for a photoshoot.

When Millie had decided that she wanted to do gym and cheer, Millie's mum had agreed to allow her to have an Instagram account to follow her friends, and to keep in touch with her gym friends who had since given up gym. In no time at all Millie had built up quite a following and had decided to answer a campaign for a new cheer clothing brand who were looking for ambassadors. To her surprise, not only had she been accepted as an ambassador, she had been invited to London for a photoshoot. This trip was to be all about family time. The first thing on the list to do was the London Eye. James really wasn't sure about going on something so big and the queues snaked all around the square. Much to their luck, a steward noticed Millie's mum's crutch and ushered them all straight to the front of the queue and straight into a pod.

"See, there are some perks to being disabled!" Mum smiled.

Since becoming ill, Millie's mum had always encouraged them all to always look on the bright side of every situation, and this was no exception. As they stepped inside all of James' reservations drifted away and excitement took its place.

"This gives a whole new meaning to flying," Millie said excitedly as they reached the top of the wheel... the top of the world. And to make it even better, they had timed it perfectly. It was just beginning to get dark as they stepped on to the wheel and as they reached the top, the sun was beginning to set and the whole of London was becoming illuminated with little lights dancing like fairies in the distance.

The following two days, the family visited the Tower of London, and again were ushered to the front of the queues thanks to Mum's crutches... the five-star treatment Mum said, although it was just as well as Millie could tell that her mum was really suffering. Millie hated seeing her mum in such pain, but she also knew that she was too stubborn to stop so knew that the best thing that she could do was help as much as possible and encourage her to take lots of breaks. After the Tower, the family had planned to go to Winter Wonderland, which Millie and James had been looking forward to most of all, but they both knew that their mum just could not manage it. They tried to hide their disappointment as they sat on the bus back to the hotel, passing what looked like the most amazing funfair that they had ever seen!

The final day was a boat trip to Greenwich where they had a look around the market and the shops, but again, Mum was struggling, and the pain was clear on her face. They cut their trip short and headed back to the car for the final time and headed for home. Not that Millie minded as she couldn't wait to get back in to gym to see her friends and tell them about her adventures.

Chapter 11

A New Year

The first day back in school, the head teacher had sent a message to Millie's mum to ask if she could represent the school in the Welsh schools' gymnastics competition... next week! Millie's mum headed straight down to the school to speak to Millie and see what she wanted to do. Knowing Millie, it would be an easy decision, but her mum had always made a point of giving her the choice to make it by herself. The first thing Millie worried about was the cost. How much would it cost her parents for her to compete?

"Never mind the cost, do you want to do it?"

Millie began to get emotional. She wanted to do it but felt like it was a waste of money. But eventually, she made her decision, she was going to represent the school. Millie only had a week to prepare, which was fine as she could just use her gymnastics floor routine, but she knew that she would have to make some big changes and wasn't sure how confident she would be competing on mats instead of a sprung floor.

On the day of the Regional schools' competition, Millie's dad drove her and her mum to the high school where it was being held. As they went to walk in to the sports hall, a teacher stopped them.

"Only pupils and teachers can come in, no parents"

Straight away, Millie's eyes began to well with tears. Millie had been entered in the competition on the understanding that her parents would take her, and so no teacher was there with her. After some persuasion, the teacher finally allowed Millie's mum in but not her dad or little Sean. Millie was beside herself with worry when she heard someone call her name. She didn't recognise her, but the girl's mum came over and introduced her daughter, Ava, who followed Millie on Instagram. Millie then heard a familiar voice call her name.

"Millie, are you ok?"

It was Katie, one of Millie's gym coaches who was there judging the competition. Katie could see that Millie was in a difficult position and that her mum was having difficulty in dealing with the situation, so she put her arm around Millie and led her towards the mat. Within minutes, Millie had regained her composure as Katie took her through a simple warm up and stretching. As the competition started, the girls gathered around the mats with their school friends. Millie, however, positioned herself on the floor right next to Katie. According to the programme, Millie was up third so at least she wouldn't have too long to wait.

As Millie took to the floor, she felt surprisingly calm and composed. She still wasn't quite sure exactly what tumbles she was going to do but would decide how it felt at the time and just go for it. And that is exactly what she did… she went for it!

As she finished her routine and took her place next to Katie, she felt pleased with her performance. She watched all the other girls, not really taking much notice of what was going on around her. Millie's mum had sat quietly at the back of the hall as instructed by the teacher on the door, watching on bored. She was sat on an uncomfortable wooden bench and was hoping that each performance was the last. Finally, the last person had performed, and everyone was looking forward to getting out of the bitterly cold hall and into the warmth of their cars. But first the results. Whoever came first overall would go on to represent the area at the National schools' competition, which would be held the following week in a small town on the west coast of Wales. As they announced the third and second places, Millie suddenly felt nervous. And as they announced Millie's name as the winner, she bounced all the way to the floor to collect her medal.

"Well done, darling," Millie's mum said after Millie had posed for photos.

"Thanks, Mum, can I have the rest of the day off school?" she asked cheekily.

"Actually, yes," Mum giggled. It took Millie a few seconds to register that her mum had said yes, and then she realised it was Thursday and it was time for gym. No rest for the wicked she thought!!

The following week at the schools' Finals was an almost near rerun of the week before, but at least this time Millie was surrounded by her family who could watch. Once again, Katie was there judging but this time there were two other judges in a more formal setting. Millie was up second to last and had to sit around the edge of the floor watching all the other girls perform. Millie couldn't help but feel bored of the monotony of the performances, and then felt bad for having such feelings as she knew everyone there was doing their best. Finally, it was Millie's turn. After the last competition, Katie had given Millie some feedback and a few ideas of things to include into her routine. Millie hadn't practised her floor routine since last week's competition, but she felt comfortable to make the new additions, and had decided to go all out on her tumbles. Normally, Millie would be quite reserved with her tumbling, having very little self-confidence and belief in herself, but since she had been doing cheer, her tumbling had grown stronger and stronger and so had her confidence. As the familiar piece of instrumental music started, Millie began to move to the beat, and straight into her first tumble, round off, flick, tuck back. Perfect! She danced she jumped, she tumbled her way across the mats and by the end of her routine, she knew that she had performed the best she could, she was happy. And she didn't even care where she came overall, she just felt proud of herself for going for it and pulling off her big tumbles on mats instead of sprung floor.

As the judges totaled up all the scores, Millie spent the time playing with her brothers. She wasn't paying any attention to the announcer who had started speaking on the microphone as he was speaking Welsh, and Millie had very limited Welsh language. Suddenly, she heard her name being called. She didn't really know what was going on but luckily Katie caught her eye and was clapping and nodding over to the mats. Millie had come third overall in Wales, not a bad achievement she thought to herself!

Chapter 12

The First Cheer Competition

With the success at the schools' competition behind her, Millie knew that she had a lot of work to put in over the next few weeks and months in both gymnastics and cheer. Coming up was ICC Wales and ICC Nationals cheer competitions and her compulsory gymnastics competition... and right in the middle of both was their family holiday to Bali. Back in gym, Millie felt happy with how everything was going. She could do all her moves and routines, all that was needed was for Millie to tidy them up.

Cheer, however, was a different thing entirely. Nationals was only two weeks away when Gina announced in training, "Girls, we are going to change the pyramid slightly, make it a little bit more difficult!"

The girls just sat and looked at each other, there wasn't really anything they could say, they just had to get on with it.

"Millie, you are going to be out the front and are going to round off flick into basket."

That's easy enough, Millie thought. They can do this! The first competition of the cheer season was at the same stadium where they had performed previously at Showcase. The day had started just as it had the last time. Hours of preparation on hair and makeup, but this time the nerves were ten-fold and very, very, real. Showcase was Millie's first official performance, but now they would be competing for real against other teams from all over Wales and England. The pressure was now on. Millie's family arrived at the stadium and met up with the girls and coaches outside to go through their team talk. Millie kissed her parents goodbye as they wished her and the girls good luck, before disappearing into the arena. Gina and Sarah told the girls to just go out and enjoy themselves, to perform exactly as they had last time in training. That was all good and well, but in training they were still having problems with one of their stunts.

After team talk, the girls made their way to the warm up area. They could hear the music pumping as the other teams performed and Millie could feel the adrenaline rising throughout her body. She stretched hard, and then had the girls stretch her some more. As the girls lined up ready to take to the stage, the nerves and adrenaline kicked in, the glare from the bright lights was disorientating and Millie suddenly felt scared. But there was nothing she could do as Lucy pulled her, waving, onto the stage. The parents all whooped and cheered for the girls as they took their positions, and Millie's mum's heart sank to the bottom of her chest... Millie's shoe lace was undone! As the music started and Millie began to tumble, all her mum could see was her white shoe lace flying. With every roar of the crowd, Millie's mum couldn't see the stunts that were being performed, all she could see was the white shoe lace flapping around, waiting for her to either trip over it, or for it to get caught.

With every movement, her mum's heart was in her mouth... waiting. And just like that it was over. The music stopped, the lights dimmed, and the crowd roared. Millie's mum had to ask the other mums how they had done, and they all giggled that all they could focus on was Millie's lace also!

As Millie ran over to her mum, she second guessed exactly what she was going to say.

"I know, I know, my shoe lace!"

All the girls giggled amongst themselves, arms around each other and happy with how they had performed. There were only a few more teams to go, so the girls sat around the floor watching and waiting for the awards to begin, cheering on the other girls from the other teams. As the last routine ended and the music had stopped, there was a sudden rush of cheerleaders heading for the floor. Millie's mum was confused as to what was going on and was feeling a little overwhelmed. She was using her crutches and was afraid of being knocked over. Luckily, she had a very protective Millie by her side.

"It's OK," shouted her mum over the din of the music and the cheers. "Go with your friends, go and enjoy yourself."

"Thanks, Mum." Millie kissed her mum and as she began to leave, she turned back. "Love you," she shouted.

"Love you too," Mum shouted back.

Millie's mum went to find the boys who were all tucked away safely, although a little bored, at the back of the stadium away from the chaos and madness around the arena floor. As Mum subsequently learned, it is a bit of a cheer tradition that you can't have an awards ceremony without a good dance party first... and they were certainly having a very good dance party. Millie's mum could see her down on the floor with all the other girls, and she couldn't help but giggle. Millie might be a fantastic gymnast, and she was also a pretty good flyer, but dance had never been her strong point. In fact, it would be safe to say that Millie had about as much grace as an elephant on a tightrope! Millie just could not dance... but she was trying! And her mum just stood and smiled. After a few more songs, it was time for the awards to be handed out. The girls all sat in a circle holding hands. Millie's heart was pumping from trying to keep up with the dance moves of the other girls, and with the excitement of the whole experience. The girls listened as the places were given out...

"In second place and a 'bid winner'... Allstars Comets"

The girls jumped to their feet and threw their arms around each other. Millie didn't quite feel the same sense of euphoria as the other girls, but she was still incredibly happy with taking second place for her first ever cheer competition. She knew that they had all performed well and knew where they needed to improve. Gina was happy with the girls, she was looking forward to getting the girls back in to the gym to start working on upgrading the stunts again... Millie's stunts, ready for ICC Nationals. What an amazing compliment that Gina had confidence in her abilities.

Chapter 13

Stepping It Up!

The first training session back, all the girls were on a high and ready to work hard! It was unusually warm for the time of year, so Gina let the girls warm up outside. There is something about a bit of sunshine that brings out the best in people. The girls were all giggly and chatted as they ran around the car park and stretched on the grass. Gina didn't mind, this was the best group of girls she had ever worked with. She had never seen a team have a bond like these girls, and she knew that they always gave their best. It didn't take long for the girls to pick up the new stunts, and Gina decided to shake it up a bit and teach them the next level of stunting. Most of the girls had private lessons to work on their tumble but Millie was already a level four tumbler thanks to her gym but stepping up the stunting was something different entirely. Stunting relied on all four members of the stunt team working together. The session was going well, and the new stunts were coming along nicely when BANG!

Millie hit the floor with such a thud that she forgot to breathe! The girls had thrown her up high into the air and

Millie slipped through the basket, landing on the back of her head. Gina went to find Gina's dad and explained what had happened. Once he got Millie home, she seemed OK in herself, although she had a bit of a headache. Millie's parents decided to keep a close eye on her and see how she was in the morning. The following day Millie still had a bad headache, both at the front and the back of her head, so to be on the safe side her dad took her up to the local hospital to get checked out. Luckily, because Millie was a child, she didn't have to wait very long before she was ushered into a small cubicle with a very odd-looking doctor, he smelled funny too! Dad began to tell the doctor what had happened, how the girls had dropped Millie from a height

"They didn't drop me," Millie interrupted, "They just didn't catch me!"

This made the doctor begin to laugh, he had never heard someone put it like that before.

"Well, young lady," the doctor began, "You very clearly have concussion. No sport of any kind for at least three weeks, although it may be longer depending on how you recover."

Yeah, like that's going to happen, Millie thought. Outside in the car park Millie turned to her dad. "I can still go to gym tonight though can't I?" Millie asked her dad quizzically.

"I think that you should have a night off tonight just to be on the safe side."

Millie sulked all the way home and locked herself away in her bedroom for the rest of the afternoon and evening. Millie's parents didn't mind, at least shut in her bedroom she was resting, which is exactly what she needed. After a few days of rest and after chatting with Millie's coaches, Millie went back to training, although she was only allowed to do light training, with Liz constantly asking how she felt and was she OK. Her head was still a bit sore but nothing that she couldn't handle. Besides, she needed to be in training as she had so much coming up.

The next few weeks whizzed by in a blur. Training in gym and cheer had been going well and Millie was feeling confident. Bring on her next competition!

Chapter 14

ICC Nationals

The final training session before Nationals was hard work. Gina pushed the girls hard and by the time training had finished, the girls were exhausted. As she walked over to her dad who was sat in the car, he could see she was looking tired. "Are you OK?" he asked.

"Yes, just tired and my head is hurting," Millie replied.

It had been a few weeks since Millie had had her little accident of the girls not catching her, but she was still suffering from headaches. She had even been sent home from school on a few occasions but with so much coming up, Millie couldn't help but feel the need to be in gym.

Despite her aches through her body and her pounding head, Millie couldn't help but feel the excitement bubbling away inside of her. Tomorrow would be her last day in school for two weeks. ICC Nationals was to be held in Nottingham which meant a lot of packing and a lot of travelling. Millie had packed her holiday suitcase, her cheer bag, hair and makeup bag, and her weekend bag. With all of that and everybody else's bags, it was certainly going to be a tight squeeze in the car.

The day started at five a.m. for the three-hour journey to Nottingham. Luckily, Millie's parents had recently bought a seven-seater car, but for this trip a bus would have been more appropriate. Millie spent the whole journey wedged in the boot seat, surrounded by bags and cases which kept falling on top of her. But she didn't mind too much because tomorrow she would be on the airplane to Bali. But first, she had to get today's competition over and done with. When they arrived, they were lucky enough to be able to park right outside thanks to Mum's disabled badge! Normally, Millie would have changed into her cheer uniform in the car, but there was just no room, so she had no choice but to lug her heavy cheer bag all the way into the arena. Inside the foyer of the arena, Millie met up with the girls, who were all ready for the day ahead. Millie and her mum looked around for the toilets, but they couldn't find them, and time was very quickly running out.

Mum shouted Millie to a small deserted corridor. "Millie come down here and get changed."

"I can't get changed here," Millie exclaimed in horror.

"Well, we can't find the toilets and you need to hurry up so if you don't get changed here, then you will just have to be late."

Millie knew her mum was tired and very irritable, and knew better than to argue with her when she was like this. In fact, Millie knew better than to argue with her mum full stop. Reluctantly, Millie headed down the corridor and hid behind an abandoned food cart. Mum stood in front of her to make sure nobody saw, although she needn't have bothered as nobody walked past anyway. With Millie in her cheer uniform, Mum now had to do her hair and makeup… in the middle of the foyer! She had curled Millie's hair the night before and secured them with hair grips so all that she needed to do this morning was to take the hair grips out and put her bow in. Mum was also becoming a bit of a pro with the makeup, so it didn't take long before Millie was made up and cheer ready. All the other girls' parents were lucky enough to be upstairs in the VIP boxes, but this being their first time here, Millie's parents hadn't known to book the VIP tickets and were in the main arena with over a thousand other parents and spectators.

"Mum, can I stay with the girls?" Millie asked.

"Yes of course, but don't leave them and we will see you in the arena after the performance"

And with a flick of her ponytail, Millie was gone, arm in arm, with the other girls. At least the mad rush of getting Millie ready meant that they wouldn't have to wait too long before the Comets would be on stage. Millie's parents and brothers fought through the crowds and filed past the ticket inspectors, and finally made it into the main arena. As they looked around, Mum started to feel a little overwhelmed. She didn't do too well in crowded places at the best of time, and this was crowded! But worse, she couldn't help but wonder how Millie was feeling. This arena had hosted some of the biggest superstars in the world, and here was Millie, getting ready to take centre stage in front of so many people. Millie on the other hand, was quite unexpectedly enjoying the experience. The warm up area was huge. There were two full size floors and plenty of space for stretching and warming up. Despite there being so many people back stage in warm up, there was still plenty of room. The holding room was a whole new experience. There was a large monitor showing the performance on the floor and soft seats. Millie really felt special, she felt like a star. And then she heard the famous words, "Next on the floor is Allstar Comets."

The crowd was deafening as the girls ran onto the floor. They had all double and triple checked Millie's laces to make sure that they were tucked in and there was no chance of them escaping. The lights were so bright that Millie could feel the heat of them beaming down on to her face. As she looked out into the audience, all she could see was a sea of people all shouting and cheering for her and her friends. This was her moment and she was going to enjoy it. The music started up and the girls tumbled into their routine. As they hit all their tumbles and every stunt, the crowd cheered and whooped! The final stunt came, and although there was a little wobble, they still made the stunt. Millie knew they had done well and as they linked arm in arm watching the performance in the playback area, they knew that wherever they came they had done their best. After their performance, the girls had a long time to wait until awards and filled their time up in the VIP boxes, watching the other teams and just enjoying the moment. The other girls used the time to catch up with old friends from previous teams, and took care to introduce Millie, although most of them knew her already from Instagram.

Time seemed to pass quickly for Millie, although it had dragged for Millie's family who had been outside trying to entertain the boys. Eventually, it was time to file back in to the arena with its pounding music to wait for the awards to begin. The girls were all taking their places on the floor for the dance party which seemed to be the highlight of the competition. By the time the awards ceremony started, all the girls were on a high. The floor was crowded with very little room to move. Their category was the largest with nineteen teams competing, and as they moved down the category the girls were getting more and more excited. They were down to the top ten and still Comets hadn't been called out. They held out until sixth position when they called out their names. Lucy and Jodie, the eldest in the team, went up to collect the trophy and the girls were more than happy, sixth at Nationals with a wobble!

But now, Millie could feel the excitement really kicking in. As she posed for a few quick photos and said goodbye to the girls, Millie's holiday had now officially started!

Chapter 15

The Holiday

Straight from Nottingham, Millie and her family headed up to Manchester where they checked in to their hotel. They would be flying early the following morning and couldn't wait to crawl in to bed after what had been a very long and very tiring day. In what seemed to be no time at all, they were all being woken up by the sound of the alarm going off. It felt like they hadn't slept, although they had all slept comfortably all night. At the airport, Millie took charge of Sean whilst Millie's parents dealt with all the usual stuff... dropping off bags and getting boarding passes. Because her mum couldn't walk too far, they had booked special assistance. Just like yesterday, Millie once again felt like a superstar, although for a very different reason. An airport worker approached with a wheelchair ready to take them through to security. The perks of having this type of assistance was that they would be able to skip all the queues at security and be whisked through secret doors into a special private lounge, where they could sit in comfort to wait for their flight.

Millie and her brothers made the most of the small kids area with a soft play space and a colouring table. They were the only children in the lounge, so they had free reign over what they wanted to do. The lady who oversaw supervising the area made a fuss of Sean and gave them sweets and chocolate. When their flight was called, the lady from before arrived to take them to the airplane as they waved goodbye to the lounge supervisor. The journey to Bali was long. It would be sixteen hours of travelling and two flights. By the time they got to the villa they were exhausted. They had been lucky enough to have a private minibus from the villa come to the pick them up at the airport. The driver arrived outside of the apartments and as he pulled back the door to let them out, Millie felt the heat of the afternoon sun touch her face. She already knew that the first thing she was going to do was jump in the pool.

As the driver held open the gate to let them into the villa garden, Millie froze. She could see people in the swimming pool. In THEIR swimming pool! It took a few more moments for it to register, and then it hit her... it was Uncle Tom!

Uncle Tom was her mum's brother, who lived in Australia, and they hadn't seen him in five years. Although they regularly spoke on Face Time, Millie had never met her two cousins, Lottie and Abigail. Millie just froze, she didn't know what to do. The feeling of happiness was just too much for her to bear and she could feel tears of happiness filling up her eyes. Uncle Tom jumped out of the pool and threw his soaking wet body around her. This was the best surprise ever.

The first few days of the holiday were relaxing, chill out days. Millie had so much fun getting to know Lottie, who was four, and Abigail, who was eighteen months. Millie's mum was so happy to see her big brother and was enjoying getting to know her soon-to-be-sister-in-law, Kate, who she had also never met. The villa itself was so big that it was bigger than Millie's house. The garden was huge and perfect for playing, and of course doing a bit of gymnastics! Liz had given Millie specific workouts that she had to do daily to keep up her strength and flexibility as her National Grades competition was less than a week after she got back from holiday. But Millie didn't mind, she made the most of the pool to do her exercises and the trees in the garden! The first week seemed to fly by. They hadn't really done very much, but they hadn't been bored either. It had been nice. And to make things even more special, the next day would be Millie's tenth birthday. Millie knew how hard her parents had saved to pay for this holiday and she was so grateful to be in such an amazing place, surrounded by her family, on her special birthday.

On the day itself, Mum had arranged a special trip out for Millie and James, they were going to the elephant sanctuary. Millie had always loved elephants, in fact she thought that they were the most amazing animals in the world. The journey to get to the elephant sanctuary was long, but Millie didn't mind, she was amazed at the huge terraces of rice growing in watery fields. She watched as the coconut farmers and their entire families were out collecting the coconuts from the trees and loading them on to rickety carts ready to take to market. As they pulled in through the gate of the sanctuary, they were greeted by the lush green of the rainforest, and then Millie heard it. Before she saw it, she heard an elephant trumpeting in the distance. She was officially in heaven. Millie ran up to the gates and tried to peer through the wire fence whilst she waited for her mum, but it was no good, there were too many plants in the way. Mum finally caught up and they were ready to go in, it was as if someone had just opened the gates of heaven. There were huge trees and large pools of water, and there they were, behind a very small wooden fence, waiting to be fed. As they got closer, Millie began to feel strangely nervous. She had known that elephants were big, but she wasn't prepared for just how big.

"Come on," said Mum, "Let's feed them."

The elephants were with their Mahouts (their keepers, each elephant has their own) who each had a wheelie bin full of fruit and sugar cane. Mum was first in, she had done this before when she had been to Thailand, so she showed Millie and James how to hold it firm and let the elephant take it with their trunk. James couldn't wait to have a go, and eventually Millie plucked up the courage to join in. At that first touch she was in love. Millie spent easily an hour feeding the elephants and would have spent longer if they hadn't been called to the pool area. It was time for them to ride the elephants. Millie and James climbed into the small wooden seat on the back of their elephant, and Mum followed behind on an elephant of her own. The elephants took them on a trek through the lush green jungle, they took in the countryside and saw the locals at work. It really was the most amazing experience of Millie's life, and all too quickly it was over, and it was time to head back to the villa. Millie smiled the whole journey back as exhaustion overwhelmed her and she fell asleep.

Back at the villa, they didn't have long to shower and get changed as they were all going out for a big family birthday celebration. It was Lottie's birthday the following day too, so it was a double celebration! As a special treat, Uncle Tom took the older three kids up to the restaurant on his moped… Lottie stood in the front by his feet, and Millie and James squeezed behind him! Not something that they would get away with back home but here it seemed to be what everybody did! Whole families piled on to small spluttering mopeds. At the restaurant, Auntie Kate had put up banners saying HAPPY BIRTHDAY EMILIE AND LOTTIE xx making it even more special. After the main course, the waitress came out with milk shakes and ice cream as a birthday treat for the kids, which the adults helped them eat. After food, Uncle Tom took the bike back to the villa whilst everyone else walked. It was dark, and the roads weren't exactly safe at the best of times, but when they walked in through the gates of the villa, Millie understood why Uncle Tom had gone ahead. Millie and Lottie walked through the gate and saw a strange flickering in the main living area. Uncle Tom was stood there with a huge birthday cake, complete with candles and sparklers. Millie felt blessed as the rest of her family sang Happy Birthday to her and Lottie. It had truly been the most special and amazing birthday ever!

With Millie's birthday over, next it was time to start celebrating Lottie's birthday, but in a cruel twist of fate they had both woken up ill. Millie had a bit of a cough, but it looked like poor Lottie had developed an ear infection and would be spending her fifth birthday in pain. The original plan had been to go to a water park, but Lottie had to stay out of the water. Instead, Uncle Tom and Auntie Kate took Lottie, Millie and James out for lunch whilst the babies were with the nanny and Mum and Dad had a chill out day by the pool.

Millie loved having some time with just them, she really felt like she was getting to know Auntie Kate and, of course, Lottie.

As a surprise that evening, the parents had arranged for a chef to come to the villa to cook for everyone. The chef asked Millie and the other kids to help, which they all really enjoyed doing. They were cooking with food that they were not familiar with but put together, it all tasted delicious. And of course, for dessert, they had birthday cake!

The rest of the week passed by in a blur of happy moments, each one as precious as the last. It wasn't long before the time came to make the tearful goodbyes. Two weeks had passed by so quickly and nobody was quite ready to go home.

Chapter 15

National Grades

Millie had been home less than a week when it was time for her National Grades gymnastics competition. She had been off school most of the week as she was still suffering from the cough which had started on holiday, although now it was getting worse! She had obviously picked up some sort of bug on holiday, but it didn't want to go away. The morning of the competition, Millie was quite relaxed. Having been away for two weeks, she knew that there was no expectation other than to go out and enjoy herself. As her mum put her hair up into a bun, Millie and Mum both thought to themselves that this was so much easier than getting ready for a cheer competition.

As they arrived at the National Institute for Sport where the competition was being held, Millie felt calm and composed. Although she had only had less than a week back in gym after her holiday, Millie felt that she was ready to go out and perform. Millie had got to the competition early to support Hayley, one of her younger team mates who was in the round before hers. As she walked into the sports hall, she caught site of a few of her old team mates dotted about amongst the spectators. She dropped her bags by an empty space where her team mates' parents were all sitting, and she was off. First, she ran over to the other side of the spectator seating and found her old team mates from City Gymnastics, and Hanna who had moved from Vale after Portugal. Next, she spotted the Welsh academy gymnasts whom she had trained with for years before they had moved to the Academy. Jeje picked her up and swung her around in the air.

Millie felt so happy seeing so many of her old friends again. As she eventually made her way back to where her parents had finally settled with the other Vale supporters, Menna and Esme, her older Vale team mates were waiting for her. She loved Menna and Esme, she looked up to them and loved them like a sister. Menna picked Millie up like a little rag doll and sat her on her hip just as she always did, and the three girls settled themselves down on the steps watching Hayley perform in her competition.

Millie didn't have too long to wait before she had to go to the lower gym for her general warm up. She enjoyed competing at the National Institute of Sport and liked that general warm up was out of the way and not too many people. It meant she could focus on her own warm up without anybody else bothering her. Once Hayley's competition was over, Millie and the other girls were walked out into the main sports hall for apparatus warm up. This was a good opportunity for Millie to also get an idea of her competitors, not that she really cared, it was more curiosity! The worst part of warm up at National competitions was the leotard change! For warm up, the girls wore sleeveless leotards, but for competition, Millie had to wear a long sleeve leotard. She loved her leotard, it was black and pink and covered in crystals, but she really, really struggled getting in to it! Millie was so tiny that she had to have a small size but getting them over her thighs and then over her broad back and chest was not exactly easy! And then there was the problem of the arms. The arms were tight leaving Millie struggling to get her arms in, but then to make things worse the arms were always too long leaving them ruffled and baggy around the wrists. Getting Millie into her leotard was a two-person job, and she didn't have long because it was nearly time for march on.

Millie marched to the floor, her first piece of apparatus, and so did her old rival, Sophie! The week before the competition, news had filtered through the grapevine that Sophie had been bragging that Millie was her only real competition. In fact, she seemed so worried by Millie that she had been telling her friends in gym that she was going to "Psych Millie out" during the competition to hope that she made a mistake. Liz had pre-warned Millie, but Millie wasn't bothered. If anything, she felt honoured that Sophie was quite obviously so scared of her, and yet she had been all happy messages on Instagram and smiles this morning. So back to floor. Because Millie's surname began with 'A' she usually ended up being first, and today was no different. Millie didn't mind though. Floor was one of her scruffier apparatus, so she was more than happier to get straight on to the floor and get it out of the way. The music started, and Millie bounced and tumbled her way around the floor. She hit every landing and made every spin. She knew herself that it wasn't as tidy as it could have been, but with having two weeks off training, she didn't expect it to be perfect, but she was happy. As she left the floor, Liz gave her high five and Sophie and the other girls clapped.

Vault was next, which again was scruffy, but she made it over which was the main thing, and she could then start to focus on bars… her favourite and the one piece that everyone expected her to perform well. Liz helped Millie with a few handstand shapes, and then she sat quietly, ignoring everything around her, mentally preparing her routine. She watched as each girl went before her, and each routine was identical, which made Millie smile to herself because she knew that her routine wasn't identical, it was harder. She had all the possible bonus moves thrown in. During the time she hurt her ankle the year previous, Millie had spent a lot of time working on much harder skills than she needed, simply because she loved bars and because she could, and now the hard work seemed to be paying off.

As Millie climbed up to the bar, she took a deep breath, wrapped her loops around the bar and dropped. She hung there for a second before swinging herself straight up in to handstand. Round and round the bar she swung before stopping. She had done exactly what she needed to do, and she knew it was good. Range and conditioning went as well as she expected. It's surprising how the shortest of breaks impacts on flexibility, so with a two-week break for something that was already a weakness, she was happy to just get through it with minimal faults. Beam was Millie's last apparatus, which normally she preferred to get over and done with, but at least today she would be fully stretched from range previous. So far, the competition had gone well so she felt very relaxed and comfortable. Sophie hadn't even spoken to her, which was surprising considering all the previous hype.

Millie stepped up to the beam and positioned the spring board perfectly where she needed it to be, turned and presented, and with a small jump, she mounted the beam. She walked and shimmied perfectly along the beam, spinning and jumping as she went. In the blink of an eye, ninety seconds had passed and her beam routine and National Grade competition was over. Millie had done everything she could, and she was happy with her performance. Only now did a flutter of nerves begin to kick in as Millie knew that the top four gymnasts would go through to compete at British Finals. Millie hadn't even thought about the possibility of qualifying but after her clean routines, maybe, just maybe, she might stand a chance of representing Wales.

As soon as the competition was over, all the gymnasts lined up on the floor ready for the medals. As the spectators all fell silent, Millie could hear a familiar noise "EEEEEEE". Her little brother, Sean, had spotted her from where he was sitting in the audience and he was shouting her. Millie stood giggling to herself as all the parents sat around Sean were cooing and making a fuss of him.

The first apparatus to be awarded was vault. Millie hadn't made top six, and she didn't on range or floor either. Next to be announced was beam, and as the announcer counted down from six through to two, Millie knew it was all over. Millie couldn't believe her ears as she then heard her name called out, she thought she was imagining it, but she wasn't, she had taken gold on beam. The last individual apparatus was bars, and inside she knew she had done well. The bonus moves had paid off and it was another gold. With two gold medals, maybe, just maybe, she would make top four... and that's exactly what she did, she took fourth overall... she had made Team Wales!

Millie was so happy it hadn't hit her when Liz took her off for photos and posted them all over social media. She had come into the competition with no expectations, and now she had managed to take two golds and would be representing Wales at British Finals.

And Sophie... she didn't even make top six!

Chapter 16

Cheer Sport Wales

A week after the success of her gymnastics National grades was Cheer Sport Wales, and the final cheer session before the competition was hard. As Millie came out of training, she looked hot and unhappy.

"How was training?" Mum asked, as Millie stepped into the car.

"Horrible!" Millie exclaimed. "Gina has been so horrible and has just been shouting at everyone all of the time."

Mum didn't say anything, she knew it wouldn't be long before Millie offered up more information, and she was right.

"She made us do like ten full outs straight after each other and all she did was shout. She changed our stunt into pyramid again and then shouted when we got it wrong. It was just horrible!"

Mum listened sympathetically. "Maybe it's just because Gina knows how much you are all capable of and is pushing you because she knows you can do it. Don't let it get to you, let's get the next few days and the competition out of the way and then we will be on a nice family holiday together."

Millie didn't respond and sat in silence the whole way home.

The day of the competition arrived and because her competition wasn't starting until late in the afternoon, Millie had gone gymnastics training in the morning. The day went by quickly because as soon as she got home from training, the whole make-over began. It was only a half hour car journey this time to the stadium, so Millie just relaxed in the back seat as she was feeling quite tired. Millie still had the cough that she picked up on holiday and had been off school most of the week. She spent most of her nights coughing and then being sick from coughing, so she wasn't just tired, she was exhausted. A few days before, her doctor had given her an asthma inhaler to see if it would help with her breathing.

Shortly after arriving Millie went into warm up whilst her parents took their seats inside the main arena. This time, it was just Mum and Dad as James and Sean had stayed at home with Grandad. Millie had been struggling in training with her breathing, but her mum had told her to take her inhaler just before they went on and hopefully it would help. During warm up, Millie stretched her body hard but didn't do too much running about. The girls went through their routine and practised a few of their stunts before doing their final checks of Millie's shoelaces, making sure that they were tucked in! The girls took their places on the floor in the centre of the arena and focused. The music began, and the girls settled themselves into their routines. The girls all seemed to be really throwing themselves into the routine, they looked to be singing and shouting all the way through. And it paid off. They nailed the performance, but as soon as the music stopped, and the girls huddled in to each other,

Millie ran off to the side to her coaches, she couldn't breathe. She took two big puffs of her inhaler and the girls helped by deep breathing with her, and very quickly she was feeling OK again, they could all go off and get their medals for participating.

The girls all went off to find their parents, and Millie did the same. She threw her arms round her mum, and then climbed onto her dad's knee, arms around his neck. Millie was just glad that it was over, she was just so tired. A few performances later came an announcement... Allstars Comets had hit zero! The girls had all worked so hard that it had showed, their routine had hit zero deductions by the judges, a huge accomplishment for the team.

The last hour and a half of the competition seemed to take forever for a very tired Millie. All she wanted to do was sleep, but the loud booming music made it very difficult and, if anything, gave her even more of a headache. She was so glad when the announcer signalled the end of the competition and the start of the dance party. Millie made her way down to the floor to join the rest of the girls, although she didn't feel very much like dancing. The first category of awards to be announced was Junior Level 2, Comets category. There were nine teams, so the girls were hopeful that they would do well. As the announcer got down to the top three, still Comets hadn't been called, so they were top three, and then top two... the girls sat in a circle all holding hands with their fingers crossed...

"And your Junior Level 2 National Champions are.... Allstars Comets!"

The girls jumped up and screamed as they gripped on to each other. Gina and Sarah both ran onto the stage screaming and joined in the jumping! The photographer managed to get the girls to calm down slightly for their photos with their banner and trophy.

The girls finally made their way to the side of the floor area where all the parents were starting to crowd. The girls posed for yet more team photos for the parents, and then individual photos in various positions with the banner and trophy. Suddenly, Gina and Sarah started screaming and jumping up and down holding on to each other. Millie looked around and didn't know what was going on. One of the mums started pushing her on to the floor, shouting, "Go! Go! Go and get your award." Millie followed the rest of the girls onto the floor where the other girls were receiving another banner and trophy.

"What's happening?" Millie asked Lucy

"We are Grand Champions!" Lucy replied.

Millie didn't really know what that meant. She had obviously heard this award being presented at all the other competitions that she had been to, but didn't know what it meant. But never mind, Millie was going to enjoy this moment just as the other girls were!!

In the car on the way home, Millie asked her mum what it meant to be Grand Champions.

"Well, it basically means that you got the highest score out of all the other junior and senior teams that competed."

"So," Millie began, "We did better than Atomic?"

"Yes, you did better in your routine than any of the other teams," Mum replied. "Do you think Gina was right now for pushing you all so hard in training on Thursday?"

"Yes, I suppose," Millie smiled.

Chapter 17

British Finals

In the time since Millie's success at National Grades and Cheer Sport, she had been working extra hard in gym ready for British Finals for the last three weeks, she had done very little cheer training as several of the girls and coaches were away in Florida at Worlds. This meant that Millie could train six days a week for the three weeks leading up to Finals. The week prior to the competition, she had had a team training session down at the Welsh Academy where the Commonwealth Games gymnasts trained. Millie already knew two of the girls as they helped in her gym, but it was still special seeing them train.

To make life easier, James stayed at home with his real dad, and Millie, her parents and Sean travelled up to Stoke the night before the competition. Millie loved staying in hotels, it always felt like an adventure, especially when there was hot chocolate in the hotel room! Millie woke early the morning of her competition thanks to a combination of excitement and nerves. She sat watching kids' TV whilst her mum and dad got some much-needed rest. Millie was so grateful for all the travelling about that her parents did with her, and besides, she loved spending some quality time with her little brother. She sat in her Wales leotard with her Wales T-shirt over the top whilst eyeing herself in the mirror. She still couldn't believe that she was here at British Finals.

Millie and her family arrived early at the sports stadium where the competition was being held. There were two rounds in each age group and Team Wales were in round two. Liz and her family were already sat in the stands as Millie's family entered the sports hall, so they headed over and sat by Liz. Millie made the most of the time to just relax as she knew she wouldn't have too long before she would have to head off with Liz to warm up. Millie watched as her other Team Wales team mates filed in, including her old coach, Julie, who looked as miserable as ever! Just as some of the other Vale gymnasts arrived, Liz turned to Millie. "Are you ready then?" Liz asked.

Millie nodded and kissed her mum, dad and Sean goodbye.

"Good luck, love you," Mum called after her.

"Love you, too," Millie shouted back as she bounced down the stairs behind Liz and out into the corridor to warm up.

At the warm up area, Liz and the other coaches lined up the girls to have their photos taken with the Wales sign and flag. Team photos were first, and all the girls had to crouch down so that they were the same height as Millie as she was so much smaller than the other three girls. Millie's mum's phone started to ping. Liz was sending all the photos through, both team photos and individual. Mum couldn't believe how grown up her baby girl was, and that they were watching her represent Wales.

Millie's competition was to start on beam. It was a steady start, a small wobble on her spin but otherwise a nice start. Floor and vault went just the same, not spectacular, but not bad either. Range was the one Millie was really dreading. The opening sequence was a pike fold up to handstand with a half turn. Now, Millie might be a good gymnast, but something that she had always really struggled with was handstands. She had always struggled to hold them, let alone all the extras added on! Before each apparatus started, there was a five-minute warm up, and Millie used this time to practice this move, but she just couldn't do it. No matter how hard she tried she just couldn't hold it! And to make things worse, Millie was up last, so she would have to sit and watch everyone else before she got up and did it herself.

The other girls were good, in fact they were very good, Millie just hoped that she didn't let the team down. Millie's mum had been filming all her routines and had also just watched her disastrous warm up. Millie was up next, and Millie's mum couldn't watch, she would record it and then watch it back later. As she took to the floor, Millie could feel the knot in her stomach rising. She took a deep breath and went for it. She leant forward and began to pike up. She hit the handstand and turned quickly. She had done it! It was scruffy, but at least she had made it and not fallen. The relief showed as Millie very coolly carried on with the rest of her routine. With that out of the way, there was only Millie's beloved bars to go.

Millie hadn't really seen anyone else's bars routine, and her mum had only seen one other person put in the bonus moves, so everyone was keeping their fingers crossed. And as expected, Millie performed her routine beautifully. But was it enough?

Millie's parents already knew how she had done as they had been tracking her scores online, but it only gave the All-Around positions, and Millie had just missed out on a placing. As the gymnasts gathered around the floor from both rounds one and two, Millie looked around, she was looking at the fifty top gymnasts in the United Kingdom at National Grade 4. Millie had absolutely no expectation going in to this competition, so when her name wasn't called for the top six, she wasn't bothered. The next medals to be awarded were the team medals. Again, none of the girls had any expectation, and neither had their coaches. In fact, the only thing that the coaches had said prior to the competition starting was to go out and have fun, and that's what they did.

The parents already knew it would be either a gold or silver medal for Team Wales, and as the announcer called out the girls for second place, they were happy beyond words. To take a silver medal at British Finals was an amazing achievement. As soon as the team medals were handed out and photos were taken, that was it, the medal ceremony was over. Millie's parents couldn't believe it, no individual medals were awarded. How would they know how she had done? But it didn't matter, the girls could celebrate a fantastic competition and a silver medal.

Sat in the car, Mum was scrolling through the pictures that Liz had put on social media, and suddenly, a new post popped up. Mum squealed. Millie had only gone and become National Grade 4 British Bars champion! She couldn't believe it, it was just such a shame that they didn't do medals for individual apparatus, but Millie was so happy, she couldn't believe that in the space of a few weeks she had become Cheer Sport Wales Grand Champion and British Gymnastics National 4 Bars Champion!

Chapter 18

Future Cheer International

After all of Millie's recent successes in gym and cheer, the hard work was very obviously beginning to show, and she was really throwing herself into her training. She knew now where she wanted to be and what she had to do to get there. Millie wanted to make Team Wales cheerleading, and she knew she had to focus on her skills and take each step as it came, taking the bad with the good. Millie had also started doing more stretching at home. This was something that she hadn't done in a long time as she spent many hours stretching in gym, but this was different. Some of the moves she needed were unique to cheer and Millie knew that the only way she would achieve them was to put in the hard work at home.

Millie's mum felt so proud of the dedication and effort that Millie was showing, and was so happy that Millie could see how both cheer and gymnastics worked together for her. The final competition of the season, Future Cheer, was just around the corner, and straight after that was team try outs. It was also quite an emotional time as the girls had built such an amazing bond with each other, and soon they would be going their separate ways with new teams. The final training session arrived, and the girls surprised Gina and Sarah with Thank You cards and gifts and special little messages, but the mums also had a little surprise for the girls. At break time, the girls all sat outside in the car park enjoying the late evening sunshine. As they were gossiping away, they didn't notice that they were suddenly surrounded by a group of parents all holding their phones out, recording. Jodie's mum was carrying eight large gift bags that she walked around handing out to the girls.

As the girls peered into their bags they began to squeal with delight, inside each bag was a Cheer Sport Wales Grand Champion jacket! The girls couldn't contain their excitement and couldn't get their jackets on quick enough. Each one was covered in different coloured crystals that shimmered in the light. Millie was in love!

Because the girls had achieved so much in such a short space of time, the parents and coaches decided that they would get the girls unique Grand Champion jackets to show how far they had come, and how proud they were of the girls, and the jackets had arrived just in time for Future Cheer!

Because Future Cheer was in Bournemouth, which was four hours away from Wales, in England, Millie's dad decided that they would make a long weekend of it and booked a caravan in a little seaside town just outside of Bournemouth. As it was going to take four hours to get there, Millie and James could finish school at one p.m., and they were so excited to be going on a road trip! They had never been to this part of England before, so they were going to make the most of it. The journey itself was long, but it was interesting. They weren't on the motorway very long before the sat nav took them through lots of winding and twisty country roads. They passed through lots of little villages, each one so very different from the last. As they pulled into the little town where they were staying, there was a huge derelict castle standing on top of a large hill looking out to the sea. Millie and James couldn't wait to get to their caravan, so they could go and explore!

As soon as they were settled and had eaten, Dad announced that they would all go out for a walk and enjoy the time being together as a family. They didn't have to walk very far before they were in the open countryside. The field they were walking across was occupied by horses and cows which were far from interested in the trespassers, and they just stood chewing the grass ignoring them as they passed by. The field they were in was high up and overlooked the whole of the bay and out to sea. Millie stood on an old crumbling mound that was once a stone wall and closed her eyes. She felt the warm breath of the evening breeze blowing around her face, and there was silence. In that moment, Millie felt content. She was happy.

After a little while, they all made their way back to the caravan as Mum's legs were not very good and she didn't want to push herself too far and then be ill for the rest of the trip. Besides, they could all do with an early night as they were having a fun filled beach day the next day. Back at the caravan, Mum busied herself making sandwiches and snacks that they would take with them for their picnic.

The following morning, Millie was the first one awake. She was so excited that she couldn't sleep, and she didn't want anybody else to sleep either. She made herself a bowl of cereal and sat outside enjoying the views as she ate. Millie tried to eat as slowly as she possibly could, but it was no use, she was too excited and there was only one thing for it, she would have to wake everyone up! James was first on the hit list, she thought at least if the two of them woke Mum and Dad up, it wouldn't be quite so bad. As Millie and James slowly opened the door to Mum and Dad's room, Millie couldn't believe it. Mum, Dad and Sean were all up, dressed and watching TV!

Mum had finished making the picnic the following evening once everyone had gone to bed, so all they needed to do was load the car up and head down to the beach. It had barely turned nine a.m. as they took their first steps onto the soft golden sand, which meant they could choose where they wanted to be without tripping over other people. They chose a spot close to the wall which was sheltered, but it was also quite close to the water. One thing that they did come to notice was that there was no tide on the part of the beach, so the sea always stayed in the same place instead of going in and out. Millie was so happy to be spending time with her family, and to be having fun playing with her brothers. Mum was just grateful to have all her family together in one place, which didn't happen very often! They spent the morning running in and out of the sea and building sand castles, and just relaxing. Once they had eaten lunch, they packed up on the beach and went for a walk along the front to see what was down by the pier.

Mum had promised that if they could find a crab line for less than £5 then they could buy one, and Dad had promised them ice cream, so they set off on a mission. They passed several ice cream sellers, but each time decided to wait until the next. Eventually, they came across a small shop which sold ice cream and crab lines, and better still, the crab lines were only £1.85 so they could get two!

As they ate their ice creams, they walked along the front taking in the view. A short distance before they reached the pier was a small museum which told them a little about the town and what it had been like in the past, but all that Millie and James were really interested in was all the souvenirs on display. As soon as there was the first mention of money, Mum ushered everybody out of the shop and back onto the street.

Next to where the museum stood was a stone launching platform for boats where a few small pockets of people were already crabbing. It seemed like a good place to try and with it being a ramp, it was safer for Sean than having a big drop. Millie and James hurriedly unwound their crab lines and couldn't wait to get them into the water, but what were they going to use as bait? They obviously hadn't thought it through very well as they had eaten most of their picnic and what was left they had taken back to the car. Mum knew it wouldn't work but suggested that they try lowering their lines into the water without bait. And just as anyone would have predicted, it didn't work! Mum asked the two girls next to them what they were using as bait and where to get some. The girls explained that they had just bought some cheap chicken pieces from the local supermarket, and it seemed to be working well for them as their bucket was full of crabs climbing over each other. Mum couldn't help but feel very disheartened, she had promised the kids they could do crab fishing, and now they wouldn't be able to do it as they had no bait, but luck was most definitely on their side.

The two girls that they had just been speaking with carried their bucket past them and down the ramp until they reached the water's edge. They counted each crab as it tumbled out of the bucket and back in to the sea. As they walked back up the ramp, they approached Millie and James.

"Would you like our crab lines, and our bait and our bucket for your crabs?"

"Yes, please," replied Millie and James in unison.

"Are you sure?" asked Mum.

"Yes of course. We came here on the bus and we don't really want to be carrying all this back home on the bus with us. You can have it. Enjoy it."

"Thank you so much," replied Millie, James and Mum one after the other.

Now, the serious crab fishing could begin! The girls had bought the more expensive larger crab lines in pink and blue, so Millie and James were quick to discard the small lines that they had been trying to use, and lowered their bait filled bags into the sea below. Mum and Dad decided to use the smaller crab lines and Sean was happy to just run between each person. The first line to come up with anything on was Mum's. A large brown crab was crawling over the bag nipping at the bits of chicken inside. Sean squealed with delight as Mum carefully removed the crab from the bag, and placed it in the bucket. For the next two hours, he sat guarding the bucket, squealing each time a new crab was landed and placed inside.

Sitting there as a family, enjoying being together, the time seemed to fly by. Millie's mum knew all too well how precious life was and these little moments were what really counted. Mum had always focused on the importance of making memories over material things, and Millie felt the same, she wouldn't swap this moment in time for anything in the world. Later that afternoon, they all headed back to the caravan for a nice relaxing evening ahead of the next day's cheer competition. James and then Millie showered whilst Mum made them all some food, and Dad chased Sean around outside on the grass. Hearing the fun and laughter from outside drifting through the bathroom window, what would normally take half an hour took Millie ten minutes as she rushed to get dry and dressed, and outside with the boys. Millie had hoped that they could go for another walk to see the horses, but Mum wasn't up to doing any more walking, and although she said to go without her, Millie would rather stay all together. Besides, they were having plenty of fun playing on the grass into the late evening, and they sat as they watched the sun setting over the sea. It was finally bed time.

Sunday morning seemed to arrive too quickly, and after the very long, busy day that they had all had the day before, Millie was not ready to wake up when Sean jumped on her, thrusting his head into hers searching for a kiss. Millie didn't have to be in Bournemouth until three p.m., and it was only a twenty-minute drive, so they decided to relax and just take the day slowly. Although they couldn't take it too easy as it would take hours to get Millie ready for her competition.

After breakfast, Millie and James took Sean outside to play on the grass, although it wasn't as warm as the day before, and they soon headed back inside. Dad switched on the TV, something they never did at home, largely because they didn't have a TV at home, and the three children sat there in silence, staring at the box on the wall. Mum decided to make the most of them being sat still and made a start on

Millie's hair. As she sat brushing and sectioning and curling, Millie didn't flinch, keeping her eyes firmly glued to the TV screen. Mum thought it was amazing how easy it was and how quickly she managed to get through her hair, typical it was the last competition of the season! Nevertheless, Mum hoped that Millie's makeup would be just as easy; but that would have been too easy!

As soon as Mum took the makeup out of its case, Sean was there. One thing he loved more than TV was makeup, and he would sit for hours pretending to have his makeup done. Every time Mum tried to do something, Millie would move as her eyes, followed by her head, would make their way back to the TV screen. In between applications, Mum would have to brush Sean's face repeatedly, letting him think he was having makeup like his big sister. Eventually, Millie was competition ready, and after the ritual of photos in various poses, they headed off down to Bournemouth. Unfortunately, so had the rest of the cheerleading world! It seemed to take forever getting in to Bournemouth itself once they had passed the "Welcome to Bournemouth" sign, and they would need a miracle to find somewhere to park. There were quite literally thousands of people in Bournemouth for the three-day International Cheer event, and every single car park was full. Normally, having a blue disabled badge would make finding parking a little easier, but not today. Finally, Dad decided to head down a few of the back streets to see if they could find anywhere, and there was just one, solitary car parking space, it had their name written all over it! And because of Mum's blue badge, they didn't have to pay either!

So, they had found somewhere to park, but they didn't know exactly where they were, or how to get to where they needed to be. They took a wild guess which way they thought the beach was and started walking. After about ten minutes, they finally hit what seemed to be civilization, and hopefully the town centre. Luckily, Bournemouth beach area isn't that big, so they followed the stream of cheerleaders who were all heading in the same direction towards a park area. By the time they had reached the park, James was complaining he was hungry, and Millie only had thirty minutes before she had to be at the arena, which looked like it was just on the other side of the park. Mum also needed to have a rest as her legs were starting to hurt, so decided that this would be the perfect time to have their packed lunch. Dad had taken control of today's picnic, and it showed. Instead of sandwiches and fruit, there were sausage rolls (that Mum had cooked the Friday they arrived) and boiled eggs still in their shells! Not to mention the crisps and sweets and packets of biscuits.

As Millie sat picking at the food, she was mesmerized by all that was going on around her. There was an orchestra playing music from the bandstand, and cheerleaders as far as the eye could see, stretching, stunting and messing around. When they finally made their way through the park, there was a man juggling fire with a sign saying, "Homeless but trying". Millie felt thankful for everything that she had, and for having her family around her. They eventually arrived at the gate to the park, one way led to the arena and the other to the beach, and this is where they would part.

Only Mum had a ticket for the actual performance as it was too long for the boys to sit and watch, and the plan had been for Dad to take the boys down to the beach to see what else was going on. Dad kissed Millie as she put her arms around him.

"Good luck," he said.

"I wish you all the luck in the world," James said as he put his arms around his sister.

Mum and Dad looked at James and couldn't help but giggle to themselves. Where on earth had that come from for an eight-year-old! But that's what they all loved about James, his randomness and quirkiness. As Millie and her mum rounded the corner to find the entrance to the stadium, the queue to get in was half way down the street. Luckily, Mum had her stick and so they walked to the front of the queue where a security guard let them pass through. Once they had cleared security and had their bags searched, the next task was to find the team rooms. Millie spotted a few of the older girls ahead of them and decided to follow them, hopefully they would be going to the same place they were. As they went up the escalator and rounded the corner, there was a sea of pink and black uniforms and a large sign saying "Allstars". They were in the right place.

In the team room were all the other Comets parents and the girls were all wearing their matching Grand Champions jackets. It didn't feel real that this would be the very last time that they would all be together. There was lots of hugging and photo taking before they all headed off to warm up together for the final time.

In the outside world, the boys had decided to head down to the beach. It was not as warm as the previous day but was comfortable. Many of the day trippers and holiday makers had started to head home, and scattered all over the sand were discarded buckets, spades and other plastic toys. James and Sean set about collecting as much as they could from the surrounding beach, one so they could play with them and two to save them being washed into the sea where they might cause harm to sea life.

Back in warm up, Millie was starting to feel sad and the nerves were setting in. The girls knew that this would be a tough competition with the best teams in the UK competing here, but they were just here to enjoy it, and that's exactly what they were going to do. The mums had all made their way into the hall ready to watch the girls perform. The hall in which the girls were competing was only small and there were hardly any spectators, which was really rubbish considering it was such a big event. The girls were due to compete in five minutes, but then it was announced that Comets would be moved to last. News started to trickle through that Danusia had been sick and fainted after coming off the floor after her performance with Atomic. Nobody really knew what was going on or if they would be able to perform. And then came the announcement "Allstars Comets", they were on! As with every routine they had performed, the girls tumbled and danced perfectly about the floor. Every tumble, and every stunt they hit, the routine was going well, and all that was left to go was the final stunt. Millie went into her round off flick and the girls caught her and swung her up into the air, and the crowd were going wild. Next was the leg change, but Kaydie missed Millie's foot as it came down and landed on her chest, followed by the rest of Millie as she fell to the ground. Millie jumped up as quick as she could, tears starting to sting her eyes as she placed her foot back into Kaydie and Lucy's hands. Up she went and grabbed Belle's outstretched hand, forcing a big smile on her face.

The music stopped and Millie dropped down in to the waiting arms of Kaydie, Lucy and Alice, the tears streaming down her face leaving black streaks as they went. The eight girls made their way from the floor with their arms wrapped around each other and headed over to the replay area. As the video of their performance replayed onto the large screen in front of them, Millie couldn't watch. She stood with her back to the screen, her head buried tightly into Jodie, and watched as the coaches stood watching, waiting for the mistake to appear.

The coaches stood smiling as they watched the replay, and then turned to the girls. Gina spoke first. "I am so incredibly proud of all of you girls. This is by far the best team I have ever had the pleasure of coaching. You have come so far and learnt so much, but you have also taught me so much along the way. You have bonded like no other team I have ever seen, and today, you fell, so what mistakes happen, but the way you have all come together afterwards is something truly special. I am really going to miss coaching you guys."

Millie looked around and everyone was crying, even Gina and Sarah. In that moment, Millie felt what it meant to be a part of something special. She had made some amazing friends whom she knew she would be friends with no matter what teams they all made next season. Straight away, the girls were ushered into an adjoining room where the awards were waiting to get under way. The girls knew that they wouldn't be up there competing for medals, but it didn't matter, they were just going to enjoy this little bit of time together. As the announcer started running down from fifteenth place, every place they thought would be theirs, all the way to sixth place when the announcer finally called their name. Sixth with a fall was amazing, it was certainly better than they had expected in a category that was so tough. They had done themselves proud.

This was the first time at an awards ceremony that there had not been a dance party, and the girls were glad. They made their way back to the team room where the parents were all waiting. Millie's mum watched as Belle's mum held Millie so tight and whispered into her ear, she could just make out, "Proud of you." Belle and Jodie's mum were both crying, it had certainly been an emotional day, and this was going to be the worst part. The girls all slowly gathered up their things and packed their bags and hugged each other in turn. Millie said goodbye to the girls as she turned to go home, her face felt hot and she was trying not to cry.

And just like that, Millie's first ever cheer season was over. She had gone into the sport as an alternative to her gymnastics, but cheer had now become part of her life. She had learnt what it meant to be a part of a team, to form bonds like no other. She had learnt to push herself further than she ever thought capable and to celebrate others achievements like they were her own.

One thing was for sure, with try outs coming up the following Sunday, Millie couldn't wait to see what the next cheer season would bring!